Black
Woods

a fantasy novel

Visit www.jack-odonnell.com to see more works written by this author.

Visit www.landoffright.com to learn more about Jack O'Donnell's Land of Fright™ series of weird tales.

Visit www.odonnell-books.com to see more works published by ODONNELL BOOKS.

AUTHOR'S NOTE

Black Woods is based on my original screenplay. I've used scene headings instead of chapter headings to give the story more of a movie-like feel.

I hope you read it with that same intent, playing out the story in the movie theater of your mind.

Hot buttered popcorn, Sno-Caps, and an Icee are optional, but highly recommended.

BLACK WOODS

The Black Woods contain darkly gnarled trees born from the seeds of sorcery, strange plants given unnatural life from the fertilizing spread of decaying magic, abnormal soil deeply contaminated with the residue of the Alchemy Wars from decades long past. Pockets of Black Woods have sprouted all over the world of Teradynea in isolated growths of midnight-black trees, most of these unexplored parcels of poisoned land still shrouded in secrecy. The tainted flora and fauna that sprout and flourish within these areas of permanent shadow contain mysterious powers that can be harvested and gathered for good. Or for evil.

What secrets do the Black Woods hold? Rin and his friend Joktala will soon discover that the Black Woods contain a hidden danger far more perilous than any they could have ever imagined...

EDGE OF THE BLACK WOODS - DAY

A figure stepped out of the deep shadows cast by the Black Woods and stood just outside the row of dark, dark trees that marked the border of these eerie, unnatural growths. This was Raker, a Volgarian.

All Volgarians were big, hulking creatures, somewhat Human in appearance. Even the smallest Volgarian male was a good six feet in height, and some of them reached nearly seven and a half feet tall. They had a slight purple-blue coloring to their flesh, as if they were born bruised all over and never recovered from it. Most Volgarian faces were splattered with warts, odd-shaped growths, and other disturbing protrusions.

Raker was grotesque in appearance, even for a Volgarian, with jagged scars ripped through his face, remnants of the dozens of brawls he had been in throughout his life. Pus-filled sebaceous cysts popped out from his flesh in half a dozen different places on his face and neck, each one threatening to burst into an oozing goo of slime at any moment.

He uncurled his fat, stunted fingers and opened his hand to stare down at two black pellets in his palm. They were tiny round pellets made of a compressed substance, barely the size of his thumbnail. He grinned a cold, evil grin as he studied the pellets, revealing his yellowing teeth, teeth discolored with irregular brown stains. He knew what the pellets contained, knew they held a simple but effective weapon formed from the right mixture of powders.

He put the pellets into a pocket on his thick wool cloak, slid his hood over his head to conceal his face, and headed away from the Black Woods.

THE VILLAGE OF FALLING STREAM
A TAKAN VILLAGE - DAY

Raker moved stealthily amongst the shadows as he headed through the Takan village of Falling Stream, moving towards the bustling marketplace he saw in the near distance. Smoke drifted up from most of the chimneys of the houses he passed, the occupants of the stone and thatch-roof houses battling the fall chill with their hearth fires.

Raker neared the marketplace. Most of the occupants of the market were Takans, as Falling Stream was predominantly a Takan enclave. The Takans were humanoid in appearance, but most of their race was smaller in stature than either Volgarians or Humans. Takans had wiry builds and exquisitely beautiful features, with a slight blue tint to their skin, a yellow gleam in their large eyes, and slightly pointed peaks to their ears. They filled the streets of Falling Stream, along with a small number of Humans as well, everyone going about their own business, oblivious of the threat that now walked amongst them.

An occasional Volgarian might be seen in a Takan marketplace, especially if he had a weakness for the Takan dewdrop ale, but it was a rare sight and one that Raker knew would call unnecessary attention to himself; he kept himself bundled in his cloak as best he could, trying to avoid being recognized. He knew his size could also give him away, but there were a few Humans who grew as tall as Volgarians, so if he was careful and kept his face and hands hidden, he knew he could at least possibly pass as a Human.

There was movement and noise coming from every direction as he drew closer to the market. A blacksmith clanged his hammer down, beating a lumpen blob of steel into something long and flat. A female Takan wandered past him, carrying a basket full of onions and potatoes. In a stall nearby, a fletcher threaded feathers into long, narrow shafts, the Takan clearly in the process of making arrows.

The smell of freshly baked bread made Raker's nose wrinkle in disgust. The Takans had the filthy habit of eating their bread straight out of a kiln. He grimaced. The bluebacks had no patience. Bread was meant to sit and ripen, letting the deliciously sour taste rise to the top, letting the green and white flavor buds blossom on its surface.

Raker hugged the black shadows of a building

as two Human males approached him. One of the males had long brown hair, the other short black hair. Raker had no idea what their Human names were, nor did he care to learn them. Wordlessly, Raker handed each of them one of the black pellets. The Humans already knew what needed to be done; they had discussed the deed a week ago in a house of dance and song that bordered the Human and Volgarian territories. Raker also handed them each a small bag that jingled with coin; they would get the rest when the job was done.

Raker quickly disappeared back into the deep shadows.

*****

On the east side of the marketplace, the brown-haired Human found a good vantage point that looked out at a group of penned mulgers.

Mulgers were tiger-like creatures that had been domesticated and trained to be riding animals. They were as long as a horse, but were much shorter in stature, much lower to the ground, much easier to mount than a horse. They had vertical distinctive stripes marking their furred bodies, an ancient vestige of the times when their breed used to hunt in the wilds of the Malarian Marshes and their stripes were used to camouflage themselves against the tall reeds that grew in those swampy lands. Over the decades of domestication, their stripes had begun to fade, but there were still lingering vestiges of their markings visible on the hides of some of the mulgers.

The brown-haired Human inserted the black pellet into a long, narrow tube that he produced from his pocket.

*****

On the west side of the marketplace, the black-haired Human male took up a position near a stack of crates, looking out at the throng of marketplace shoppers. He, too, pulled out a long, thin tube from his waist, eyeing several mulgers nearby as he did so.

*****

The brown-haired Human slit his finger with a dagger, let a few drops of blood drip into the tube, then quickly put the tube to his lips. He blew hard and fast into the tube, firing his weapon, sending the black pellet rocketing towards the penned mulgers.

*****

The black-haired Human loaded his pellet, taking aim at the mulgers near him. He bit his cheek and spit blood into the tube, then fired, exhaling a sharp grunting breath to propel the pellet forward with a burst of velocity.

*****

The black pellets soared through the air, transforming as they flew, the blood acting as a trigger mechanism, turning the black pellet balls into tiny black spyflyers.

Spyflyers were spider-like creatures with nasty, hooked claws on the ends of their eight spindly legs, and one razor-tipped stinger that jutted out from the bottom of their abdomens. They unfurled from their pellet shells as they flew through the air, spreading out, lengthening to about two inches.

One of the spyflyers hit a mulger and grabbed hold, sinking all eight of its claws into the mulger's hide, then immediately plunging its stinger into the mulger's flesh!

The second spyflyer hit another mulger, brutally stinging it, sending its stinger deep into the mulger's side, spreading its pain-inducing poison with a quick ejaculating squirt.

The two stricken mulgers howled in agonized unison, both of the animals shrieking in pain and howling with fright. They bucked and kicked, futilely trying to dislodge the viciously attacking source of their intense pain.

And then all of the mulgers went berserk as the fear spread like a contagion. Every mulger nearby, three dozen at least, began howling, jumping up and down, twisting and turning wildly! They ripped free of their bindings and began rampaging through the marketplace, overturning carts, trampling wares in their mad uncontrollable dash to flee the area.

A mulger bucked and kicked, striking a Takan female in the head with its deadly hooves, sending her crashing to the ground as blood streamed out of the gash in her head.

Another mulger ripped its reins free of its post

and raced away, trampling two young Takans who were unfortunate enough to be in its path, the hard hooves of the beast tearing into their blue-hued flesh as it ran over them.

Another group of mulgers stampeded down a narrow side street. The four Takans heading towards the marketplace on that narrow street had nowhere to flee; the mulgers ran right through them and over them, killing two of them instantly and inflecting enough damage on the other two Takans that they would die within hours.

Dozens of Takans fell victim to the mad, uncontrollable stampede of the fear-struck mulgers.

*****

Just outside the village, Raker paused to lower his hood and listen to the screams of the dying. He smiled his cold, evil smile, raised his hood back up over his head, and continued on his way.

EDGE OF GREYSTONE
A HUMAN VILLAGE JUST BEYOND TAKAN
TERRITORY - NIGHT

The orange glow of a torch burning hotly in the night cast a small circle of light. The torch was being carried by Rin Grinto, a male Takan. As with all Takans, Rin had a wiry build and exquisitely handsome features. Rin held the torch out before him as he walked and the light illuminated the slight blue tint to his skin, the yellow gleam of his eyes, the pointed peaks of his ears. And the sadness in his face. "I just miss him, you know," Rin said. "I didn't even get to go to his burial."

Walking next to Rin was his friend, Joktala Sleestaka, also a Takan, but with skin of a much darker blue than Rin's. Joktala had a bow slung over his shoulder. They were both dressed in tunics, breeches, and leather boots. "It's not your fault you were ten sunrises away when your father died, Rin," Joktala said.

"Yes, it is. Every time I go away on one of my soul-searches, something bad happens."

Joktala shook his head. "It was a freak accident. Those mulgers just went berserk. They trampled fifteen Clan members before they were killed."

Rin nodded, but guilt clearly still covered his face. He pulled a sparkling green gem from his pocket and turned it over and over in his hand. "I didn't even get to give him a Luckstone for the Journey."

"Alaysia gave him one," Joktala said.

Rin scoffed. "Alaysia." He put the green gem back into his pocket. "When I came back, she handed me a sack full of my clothes and kissed my cheek. Bye bye, Rin. Lose your father, your lover all in less than half a moon's rise." Rin paused. "And I still don't know where my mother is." Rin shook his head.

"She'll come back. You know she will."

Rin lifted his head, his hope clearly building in the expectant look in his eyes. "Do you think so?"

Joktala nodded. "Come on, Rin. I lost track of how many times your mother's pulled her disappearing trick."

Rin dropped his head. "Yeah, my mother," he muttered, the dejection clearly audible despite the softness to his voice.

"Your mother's pretty outspoken for a Clan female," Joktala said. "I'm surprised the Council lets her get away with it. She's starting to attract a few powerful followers." Joktala paused for a moment. "I, for one, have to agree about what she says about the Volgarians. We should completely restrict their entry into Takan territories. They're all just a bunch of knobby-head, pus-faced savages."

Rin said nothing.

Joktala stopped walking, noticing his friend's glum face. He adjusted the bow slung over his shoulder, then dug into a pouch at his waist and pulled out a small green leaf. "Here, have some sweet leaf." The leaf was a very dark green with a series of light red, nearly pink, veins branching out along its flat surface. It was oval in shape with a rounded top half as wide as its bottom; a tiny bit of stem was still attached at the bottom of the leaf.

Rin refused the leaf with a quick shake of his head. He looked at his friend with a slight frown. "I thought you said you were going to quit the leaf."

"I can quit any time I want." Joktala grinned. "I just don't want." Joktala popped the leaf into his mouth and it had an immediate intoxicating effect on the Takan. A new, wild energy filled Joktala's face as the leaf's influence took hold. He suddenly burst out into an impromptu song and resumed walking as he sang boisterously. "We're gonna get some Human tonight. They'll be hairy but that's all right. They'll moan when they cream, and we'll think it's just a dream. We're gonna get some Human tonight."

A deeper frown creased Rin's lips as he moved to catch up to Joktala. "Wait a minute. Humans? You never said anything about Humans."

Joktala grinned slyly, pausing in his walk to leer at his friend. "Oh, did I forget to mention that?" Joktala pulled out another leaf from his pouch and rubbed it between his fingers. He motioned for Rin to take it. "It'll make the Humans taste better."

Rin squinted curiously at his friend. "Taste better?"

Joktala nodded. "Yeah. They like it when you lick 'em. Then they'll do anything for you. And I mean anything."

Rin scrunched up his face. "I'm not licking any Human. I don't care what she'll do to me."

Joktala looked at the sweet leaf in his hand for a moment, shrugged, then popped it into his mouth to join the other.

Around them, the night was quiet as they walked, each lost in their own thoughts. A slight breeze blew through the trees, the soft wind making the trees rustle with faint noises.

A treebiter, a small squirrel-like animal with a rat-like tail, lazily chewed on the bark of a nearby tree as the two Takans walked past, sinking its sharp, but very tiny teeth, into the hard trunk and moving its jaws quickly back and forth, grinding off a piece of the bark to feed upon. It was a common animal in this area, so the Takans paid it no heed, nor did the treebiter think much of their presence.

In the trees above, gryfwings leaped from tree to tree. The gryfwings were tiny, sleek-bodied animals about a foot to two feet long with short, stunted wings that they used in quick, flapping bursts to get them from branch to branch. The gryfwings were covered in a hairless sheen of smooth flesh and they had long sinewy tails they used to grip tree branches with as they moved. They, too, were a common sight in this area.

"Alaysia used to like to take walks at night," Rin said, muttering the words as if they were just an unimportant afterthought.

Joktala scratched his cheek, clearing thinking about something but not quite sure how to say it. "Listen, Rin—"

Suddenly, Rin stopped abruptly, peering down at something on the ground. He crouched down for a closer look, bringing the burning torch lower to the ground to reveal a dark wet smear of something staining the earth.

"What is it?" Joktala asked, peering down over Rin's shoulder.

Rin looked back up at his companion. "Blood. Smells Human. It's definitely not Takan. Could be from some animal. It does smell Human to me, though. It's got that same coppery smell I remember from that time that Human cut himself up in the marketplace and splashed his blood everywhere."

"Maybe one of them was in her cycle or something," Joktala said. "They bleed every full moon, you know. Something to do with their breeding cycle."

Rin frowned at Joktala. "I don't think they just let themselves bleed out on the ground." Rin stood, raising the torch higher to follow the drops of blood. He moved towards a row of dark, thick trees in the distance.

The trail of blood led up to the edge of the woods, then disappeared into the darkness beyond.

Rin stared with growing nervousness at this pocket of Black Woods. The bark on all of the trees was jet black, darker than a shadow's shadow. Visibility into the trees dropped off abruptly at the edge of the torch's light. The woods were ominously, eerily quiet. "They went into some Black Woods," Rin muttered softly, more to himself than to his friend.

"Let's see where it leads," Joktala said.

Joktala continued walking.

Rin went no further, stopping a few feet away from the edge of the Black Woods as anxiety, and what could be fear, crept into his eyes.

Joktala stopped, looking back at his friend. He glanced at the Black Woods, then back to his friend. Disbelief and amusement flooded Joktala's face. "Don't tell me you believe in all those Black Woods' myths? They're just stories to scare younglings."

"Have you ever gone in any Black Woods?"

"No." Joktala quickly added, "I never had a reason to before."

Just then, strange noises drifted out of the Black Woods, animalistic snarling and grunting, unsettling sounds to the two Takans.

"Yeah, well, you know those stories?" Rin asked rhetorically. "They worked on me." He handed the burning torch to Joktala. "You can tell me what you find."

Joktala shook his head disappointedly at Rin, then looked at the Black Woods. The torchlight spilled into the Black Woods for a few feet, but then suddenly stopped as if it was too weak to overcome the deep blackness beyond. Joktala watched with widening eyes as the blackness seemed to creep closer, devouring more and more of the torchlight with each passing moment. He glanced at the torch, to see if perhaps the flame was dying, but the fire burned just as hotly as before. He glanced back into the Black Woods. It was as if there was something blocking the light from penetrating any deeper into the Black Woods, or as if there was something within the Black Woods devouring the very light itself.

"Aren't you going in?" Rin asked, cocking his head with a hint of mockery in his tone.

"Hey, you don't know if it's Human blood for sure," Joktala said. "It could be—"

"AAYEEEII!" Something came charging out of the Black Woods, screeching wildly!

Joktala and Rin nearly jumped out of their boots as the dark shape raced past them!

The shape quickly lost speed, stumbled, and fell to the ground, sending a smattering of leaves and dirt and twigs fluttering up into the air as it hit the ground with a thud. Then, the shape lay still.

Rin and Joktala stood motionless for a moment, slowly catching their breath. They stared at the inert shape of what looked like a body for a long moment, neither of them saying a word. Finally, they took hesitant steps towards the fallen figure.

Rin took the torch back from Joktala as they moved closer to the fallen body. "Do you smell it?" he asked Joktala, but didn't really need an answer. He reached the shape first and his face filled with disbelief and disgust. Rin looked over at Joktala. "Myths, huh?"

Joktala joined him, grimacing at what lay at their feet, scowling down at the form of a Human female. The only thing she wore was a dark sheet of blood covering her otherwise naked body. Savage bruises, darkly purple, were spread up and down the insides of both thighs. Her lower lip had been nearly chewed off completely. Her eyes were open and glassy, eerily reflecting the torchlight.

"I think it's Human," Rin said. "Or at least it used to be."

Joktala studied the Human female for a moment, moving in closer for a better look.

And then she abruptly sat up!

Rin and Joktala leapt back, their eyes wide with surprise and alarm. "Elders curse me!" they both cried out in frightened unison.

The Human female stared blankly at her surroundings for a moment, slowly getting her bearings. She saw the two Takans staring at her and a fresh rush of urgency suddenly filled her face, but her words came out in a halting, hesitant jumble. "Takans. You have to stop them. They're planning to... it's... horrible. I saw it. I saw... I saw... I saw..."

Rin and Joktala said nothing. She was clearly having difficulty speaking because of her chewed lip and her disoriented state, but the Takans let the Human continue to talk, not knowing what to make of her ramblings.

"I wanted to... warn your people..." the Human said. "They're using the Black Woods... I saw... I saw... I saw..." The female gasped for a breath, then once again fell to the ground to lay still. Her chest stopped rising and falling.

Joktala took a step closer and stared down at the Human female for a long moment. His gaze moved over her body, lingering at her nether regions. "I told you they were hairy."

POWDERKEEPER SHOP
BORDERING HUMAN AND TAKAN
TERRITORY - NIGHT

Lizette McRee, a pretty, young Human female in her mid-twenties, moved down a narrow alley and stopped just outside a nondescript doorway hidden in the heart of the alley. She had sleek black hair that hung down past her shoulders, a strong face with prominent cheekbones, an aquiline nose, and a slight cleft in her chin. There was a toughness to her features, a hardness in her demeanor, but her physical appearance was often in contrast to the insecurity and self-doubt that hampered her throughout her life. She looked tough, but she didn't always feel that way.

The dimly lit doorway where she had stopped was the entrance to the PowderKeeper's shop. PowderKeepers were tolerated, but not respected nor liked, in some Human villages as long as they remained hidden in remote sections of town or in lightly-traveled areas. The wares they sold were not held in high regard by many Humans. Many people believed their goods to be fake, harmless concoctions created for the gullible, their supposed effects just imaginary and without true power.

Others thought differently because they had seen the effects of some of the goods the PowderKeepers sold first hand. Lizette was one of those others.

Lizette paused before the door, uncertainty filling her face. Then a firm resolve replaced the hesitancy. "Now's not the time to wet your pants, coward," Lizette muttered to no one but herself. She glanced both ways up and down the alley, then pushed the door open and disappeared inside.

Lizette moved into the PowderKeeper shop, studying her surroundings. The walls of this small store were lined with wood shelves, each shelf filled with glass jars containing powders of all kinds, each powder a different texture and color. Some of the powders had a crystalline look to them, while others were finely ground into grains even finer than the sands on the shore near Crystal Falls. Some of the powders were a vibrant yellow, some a muted red, some a dullish grey, others white or even black. Some of the glass jars contained pre-mixed powders, their multi-hued contents ready for immediate use without additional ingredients required.

A few small creatures, the Gatherers, moved amidst the shelves and jars, a few of them cleaning the shelves with their tails, using them as dusters. Gatherers were simian-like animals with a round fluff of fur framing their intelligent faces. They had slender fur-covered arms nearly twice as long as their fur-covered legs. The largest of the Gatherers was only about two feet tall. Other Gatherers were seeing to the contents of the jars, raising them to steady them or mixing powders together to create new products to be sold.

One Gatherer made a chittering sound that was clearly a sound of disapproval as he looked at the contents of a jar. He gave the jar to a second Gatherer who gripped the jar in his long slender fingers and then expertly bound from shelf to shelf with tiny hops as he headed through a Gatherer-sized hole that led into a back room.

Then the door behind the counter opened and a PowderKeeper stepped into the room. But it wasn't really a step. It was more like a glide as PowderKeepers didn't have feet. They had a rectangular, almost tree-trunk-like torso that led to a flat singular foot. Beneath this base of flesh that served as their foot, dozens of what could be called toes propelled the creature, as if these toes were really dozens of little scurrying legs jutting out from the bottom of their foot. The PowderKeeper was somewhat humanoid in his facial appearance and had a thick growth of reddish hair atop of his head, but he was still a strange-looking, multi-armed creature with a small mouth and disturbing, beady eyes. Instead of fingers, the PowderKeeper had a dozen tendrils extending from the end of each of his four arms. The tendrils weaved excitedly through the air as he spoke. "Want?" The PowderKeeper's voice was deep and a bit ominous.

Lizette stared at the strange creature for a moment, then forced herself to respond. She had only seen PowderKeepers a few times before and their weird appearance always caught her off guard at first. "Ice daggers and fire blades." Lizette moved quickly up to the low shelf in the back of the room and dug into a pouch secured around her waist to pull out a few dirty gold coins. She dropped the coins on the counter and they jangled as they hit the scarred wood of the countertop. "As many as my coins will buy."

Two Gatherers instantly appeared, scurrying along the counter up to the coins. Lizette backed away, apprehensive at the flurry of activity and the chattering noises the Gatherers made as they scooped up her coins. The small monkey-like creatures took the money into their tiny hands, each one only able to hold three or four coins at most, and disappeared into the back room through another Gatherer-sized hole near the door where the PowderKeeper had entered.

"Why?" the PowderKeeper asked.

"I ran out," Lizette said.

The PowderKeeper blinked very slowly. He stopped waving his tentacle arms and they went limp at his side. His beady eyes stayed focused on Lizette. "Why?"

Lizette frowned. "For protection."

The PowderKeeper's tentacles whipped about, wriggling and writhing in the air. "Who want hurt little human girl-thing?"

The quick movement of the PowderKeeper's tentacles startled Lizette, but that surprise quickly turned to an aggravation that could be clearly read on her face. "What's with the twenty questions? Can I have them or not?"

The PowderKeeper again blinked very slowly, slowing the motion of his tentacle arms. "Who want hurt little human girl-thing?"

Lizette gritted her teeth. "Look, Keeper, I ran into a little trouble. I just need something to defend myself with."

The PowderKeeper stared at her, his beady eyes dilating wide then narrowing to near pinpoints. "Ice daggers, fire blades kill, not defend. Ice daggers, fire blades kill many. Why little human girl-thing want to kill many?"

Lizette forced herself to stay calm, though it was obvious she was ready to explode with impatience at any moment. "None of your business."

The PowderKeeper blinked slowly. "Your business is my business. You not tell. I find out."

Suddenly, three thin tendrils shot out from beneath the PowderKeeper's mop of red hair and attached themselves to Lizette's head, one on each temple and the third square in the middle of her forehead. She gasped, then was quiet and completely still, her eyes closing almost peacefully. In that brief moment of calmness and serenity on Lizette's face, it was quite apparent there was a beautiful girl hidden beneath the grime and sweat. Then, with a jolt she gasped again, her eyes going wide!

THE KINTOEL TAVERN – A HUMAN-OWNED
ESTABLISHMENT – NIGHT
LIZETTE'S MEMORIES

A dream-like haze filtered everything as the PowderKeeper moved through Lizette's memories, surfacing different images, sounds, smells. A sleazy tavern filled with raucous patrons came into focus. The tavern's patrons, all male but for a very few females, were a mixed bag of Humans and Volgarians. Swirling clouds of smoke, some a reddish-pink, some brown, some white, filled the large room, drifting up from pipes of all shapes and sizes. Several Human females moved amongst the predominantly male crowd, bringing frothy foam-topped drinks or re-fills for their pipes; one human female moved through the crowd with a tiny fire-tipped stick, lighting pipes that had gone out.

The PowderKeeper observed all this through Lizette's eyes, through her memories of the place, through her memories of all the activities that had gone on around her.

Lizette was on the stage in the middle of the room, obviously one of the performers in this fine establishment. The stage was a round platform about ten feet in diameter with a worn leather floor. The platform was raised up about three feet off the ground to give everyone in the tavern a somewhat decent view of the stage's occupants. Two small sets of stairs were positioned on opposite sides of the platform to give the performers access to the stage from different directions. Numerous mirrors were positioned about the stage, giving the audience several opportunities to view the action on the stage from different angles without leaving the comfort of their chairs. One reflection revealed Lizette dressed in a tight-fitting red dress that hugged her hips and her breasts. Her expression was flat, not unhappy yet not happy either, the face of someone who had done this dozens, if not hundreds, of times before and was trying to force her enthusiasm to the surface but wasn't quite succeeding.

Another Human female, Noreena, moved up one of the sets of stairs to join Lizette on the stage. Soft trails of smoke coming from the pipes of numerous tavern patrons swirled around her as she moved. Noreena was a busty redhead with mesmerizing green eyes. She had a round face with just a hint of cheekbones showing through, a softly rounded chin, and a very sensuous mouth. She wore a sheer green slip of a dress buttoned all the way up to her slender throat that left little to the imagination, revealing a hint of the dark circle of her nipples beneath the thin silky fabric, and a tantalizing glimpse of the dark bushy growth of her femininity.

Lizette extended her hand and helped Noreena up the steps. She gave Noreena a warm, but tired, smile and the two Human females embraced in the center of the stage, pressing their breasts firmly against each other. They kissed passionately.

The crowd went wild, shouting and jeering at the performers.

Noreena began to slowly undress Lizette, teasingly, very slowly undoing the top button on her bodice.

OUTSIDE THE KINTOEL TAVERN – A HUMAN-OWNED ESTABLISHMENT – NIGHT LIZETTE'S MEMORIES

The PowderKeeper continued his probe, moving through Lizette's mind, searching.

Lizette and Noreena left the tavern for the night, heading for their mulgers, the tiger-like creatures that went berserk earlier in the Takan village of Falling Stream. The animals were attached to posts a few yards down the street. The night was calm, with just a hint of a breeze ruffling their hair. The smell of roasting meat coming from the tavern's kitchen mingled with the smell of pipe smoke that drifted out from the door.

Suddenly, four Volgarians appeared out of the night's shadows, the big hulking males surrounding the two Human females. One of the Volgarians had a cold, evil grin on his face. It was Raker, the Volgarian who was responsible for the mulger stampede in the marketplace. Raker's face seemed even more grotesque in the moonlight, with the scars ripped through his purplish-blue face glowing in the orange-white light, and the pus-filled protrusions jutting out from his flesh seemed to throb as moon shadows flicked over and around them. His voice was thickly slurred from a night of heavy drinking, his words deep and guttural from a throat dried by heavy smoking. "You come with us." He stepped forward, reaching for Lizette.

Lizette and Noreena backed away from them, Lizette twisting her shoulder to avoid Raker's groping hand. Lizette grabbed at Noreena's hand, clutching her friend's fingers tight.

Noreena waved her free hand dismissively at the Volgarian. "Beat it, knobby head." Despite her show of bravado, there was clearly fear in Noreena's eyes.

"You two are mine now," Raker said. "I want to play with you." Raker rubbed his groin obscenely, his bulge making grotesque pulsing movements beneath his stained breeches.

Noreena frowned, her lips setting tight. "What the hell are you talking about? Leave us alone."

"You are mine now," Raker said.

"Go play with your Volgarian bitches," Noreena snapped.

One of the other Volgarians belched grotesquely and spit out what came up with it. The other Volgarians exchanged looks and laughed uproariously.

"We want a private show," Raker said.

Time seemed to slow down as the brutish creatures surged forward, lunging at the females. Everything that followed moved in a nightmarish haze. In her haste to flee, and in her true fear of Raker's demand, Lizette pushed Noreena out of her way. Was it an accidental push or a deliberate shove? The action played itself out over and over again in her memory, sometimes with just an ever-so-gentle nudge that made Noreena stumble, then sometimes with a brutally violent shove that sent Noreena crashing hard to the ground. The action played out again and again in her mind with different variations in between that gentle bump and that harsh shove. Regardless of how the push actually happened, it always ended up with Noreena stumbling and going down, her body floating to the ground in a seemingly endless fall.

Lizette looked down at her fallen friend to see Noreena raising her hand out to her, her green eyes beseeching her for help.

"Lizette!" Noreena cried out.

Lizette hesitated a moment, looking down at her fallen friend, at her outstretched hand. She glanced up to see the Volgarians shouting at her, their already grotesque faces twisted and distorted into hellish masks, all of them with frightening, twitching bulges writhing beneath their soiled breeches.

"Lizette!" Noreen's cry for help seemed to go on forever, the word lingering in the air for what seemed like hours.

The Volgarian faces loomed larger, the shifting moon shadows turning them into truly monstrous visions from the worst nightmare she could ever imagine; their obscene bulges continued to pulse and throb and writhe, straining against their breeches.

Lizette turned and ran, fleeing into the night.

24

Behind her, Noreena screamed, the sounds horrible and loud in Lizette's ears, echoing over and over again inside her mind.

POWDERKEEPER SHOP
BORDERING HUMAN AND TAKAN
TERRITORY - NIGHT

The tendrils released from Lizette's head with a soft sucking noise and disappeared back into the PowderKeeper's hair.

Lizette was immediately alert, glaring hotly at the Keeper. "What did you do to me, you son of a bitch!" She clutched at her forehead, rubbing the spot where one of the tendrils had attached to her flesh.

The PowderKeeper showed no emotion as he responded. "Only truth get you what you need."

"I'm gonna butcher me some Volgarian trash!" Lizette said, sharply snapping out the words. "They took Noreena and they're gonna pay for it! You got a problem with that?"

The PowderKeeper emitted a shrill whistle from his tiny mouth and the shop erupted into a frenzy of activity with Gatherers leaping from shelf to shelf, plucking various jars from the shelves, bringing them over to a small platform near the counter. They efficiently mixed the powders, opening the jars to get the proper amount of ingredients from each. One of the Gatherers combined a drop of one yellow powder with a dark blue powder, then sprinkled a dash of a black powder into the mix. Another Gatherer poured a heaping helping of a dark red powder onto the mixing platform, then mixed it with a portion of a white powder. Both Gatherers used a tiny wooden spoon to mix the powders into the proper formulations. Once they were satisfied with their mixes, the Gatherers made a similar chittering sound which caused two other Gatherers to produce some tiny vials.

Quickly, four tiny vials were brought to the PowderKeeper, two filled with a blue powder, two with red, the powders filling the vials nearly full; The Gatherers left some room in each vial for a topper to seal them off. The PowderKeeper dipped a tendril into each vial simultaneously, somehow testing them all at once by just touching them with his tendrils. Satisfied, he sealed them each with a cork. He handed the vials back to the Gatherers and the Gatherers tapped the cork tops down a little more firmly into place with the backs of their spoons, giving the corks a few good whacks to lodge them into place.

"Wear human-thing-covering over human-thing hands. Hands no freeze. Hands no burn," the PowderKeeper said.

Lizette looked at the vials dubiously. "That's it? That's them?"

"You smear on steel blade. One vial, one blade. When powders kiss steel, steel make powders come to life. Blue ice. Red fire." The PowderKeeper blinked slowly. "Easy to keep straight. Even for little human-girl thing."

"How long do they last?" Lizette asked.

"One hour," the PowderKeeper replied. "Some more. Some less." All of his tentacles raised up into the air, then lowered, and Lizette wondered if that was supposed to be a PowderKeeper version of a shrug.

Lizette took the tiny glass vials from the Gatherers and looked at them for a long moment, studying the seemingly innocent batches of fine grains, then pocketed them. She looked up at the PowderKeeper, the lines in her face taut, her lips tight. "If they don't work, I'm coming back for you."

"They work," the PowderKeeper said. "You come back. Pull your lips back and show teeth to me. Buy more powders. Send little human girl-thing friends with more coin."

Lizette glared at the PowderKeeper but said nothing more.

EDGE OF GREYSTONE
A HUMAN VILLAGE JUST BEYOND TAKAN
TERRITORY - NIGHT

Rin rose up away from the dead Human female, the pungent smell of her coppery blood still stinging in his nostrils. He quickly scanned the surrounding area, the thick growth of Black Woods before them, looking for signs of a possible attacker, but seeing nothing. He looked back down at the dead female, shifting the torch away from her so the light revealed less of the garish evidence of wounds inflicted upon her flesh. "What do you think she was talking about?"

"Do you expect me to understand her?" Joktala asked.

"You're the one with a thing for Human females, not me," Rin said.

"I never said I understood them. I just like to play with them." Joktala glanced up and saw a large, ominous structure in the distance, a large, multi-storied house hidden in the stretch of normal woods that flanked the darker growth of Black Woods. "Hey! There it is! I knew it was around here somewhere."

"Is that the house you were talking about?" Rin asked.

"Yeah. But I told you I haven't been here for a while." Joktala glanced back down at the corpse. "I think there's been a few changes to the neighborhood." He looked over at the nearby growth of Black Woods. "Those Black Woods look a lot closer to the house than I remember them being." Joktala hesitated for a moment, staring at the Black Woods, then looked away from the dark trees. He moved towards the house.

Rin pointed to the dead female. "What about her? We can't just leave her here."

Joktala shrugged. "Rin, she's just a Human."

HOME OF HUMAN JASON ALEXIAN - NIGHT

Rin and Joktala reached the front door and suddenly stopped, seeing that the door was open. Rin glanced at the slight opening, frowning at the deep crack of shadow thrown by the heavy wooden door. "I believe that means stay away."

Joktala ignored his warning and stepped past Rin, pushing the door wider, moving into the house. Rin followed close behind.

Torches hanging from sconces on the walls illuminated the house in an orange-red light. The flames crackled and danced as the inflow of fresh air from the outside made them flare up. Just inside the foyer of the house, the two Takans saw a stairway before them, the wooden steps rising up to a landing on the next level that led to various rooms on the far side of the landing. "We can reach the Human's council chambers in two hours," Rin said. "Let them know one of their kind is dead."

Joktala frowned. "And how do we explain why we are out here in the Human territories? You want to tell them we've got a taste for their females?"

"*You've* got a taste for their females, remember?"

Joktala ignored his friend's interjection. They moved deeper into the house, walking slowly, turning their heads side to side with nearly every step. "This place used to be crawling with Humans. I don't get it."

Suddenly, a shrill scream ripped through the house! Both of the Takans froze for a brief moment, then quickly recovered.

"I hate that!" Rin exclaimed.

"It came from upstairs." Joktala pointed to the torch in Rin's hand. "Get rid of that thing. You'll give us away." He kept his voice low, hushed.

Rin moved back to the front door and tossed the torch outside into a patch of dirt, then quickly moved back to Joktala. The two Takans moved cautiously forward towards the source of the cry, easing their way slowly up the wooden stairs. One of the stairs creaked loudly as Joktala put his weight on it and he froze. Rin froze as well and they both remained motionless for a moment, listening. After another moment, Joktala continued on moving up the stairs, gripping the edge of his bow with one hand as he moved. Rin stepped wide over the creaking stair, avoiding it entirely.

Rin and Joktala reached the top of the stairs and headed down the long hallway, moving much slower now. Joktala pressed his bow into Rin's side, stopping him. "I hear voices," he whispered.

They paused and held themselves still, listening. They heard voices coming from the room at the end of the hall. The door was ajar and they could hear deep, gruff voices emanating from within the room.

Fear flashed across Rin's face. "Volgarians."

"You sure?" Joktala scowled. "What are they doing here?

Rin stared down the hallway for a moment, pondering the implications of what they were doing. Then, another chilling scream pierced the air. He turned to Joktala. "This isn't our problem," he whispered. Rin turned and began heading back towards the stairs.

Joktala's face filled with determination. "I hate Volgarians." Joktala eased forward, walking quietly and carefully. He popped another sweet leaf into his mouth and chewed vigorously.

Rin turned back to stare at his friend for a moment, then followed Joktala with a begrudging frown wrinkling his mouth. He drew a throwing dagger from his boot as he neared his friend, feeling the reassuring strength of the wooden handle in his hand as he gripped the weapon. "I thought you were bringing me out here to have some fun," he whispered.

Joktala shot Rin a cool stare and a sly grin. "You mean this isn't fun?"

They reached the open door at the end of the hallway and Joktala cautiously peered inside to see several cowering Human females crouching amidst several Volgarians. All of the Humans were splattered with blood, their hands bound with ropes. One of the Human females was on her hands and knees, with a Volgarian mounted behind her thrusting his torso against her backside again and again. Several Human females also lay motionless on the floor in a corner, and appeared to be dead. Most of them were without any clothing covering their forms.

One of the naked females who was on her knees near the middle of the room glanced up and saw Joktala staring at her from the doorway. Unbeknownst to the two Takans, she was Lizette's captured friend Noreena. Joktala could see her face overflowing with sheer terror. Her lips moved but he could not hear her say "Help me" as she mouthed it silently.

Joktala quickly turned back to Rin. "They've got them all tied up." He kept his voice low, hushed, but there was an obvious tone of alarm and urgency to his words.

"What?"

"The Volgarians," Joktala said. "They have all the Humans tied up. There's blood everywhere."

Joktala turned back to the room to see Raker the Volgarian staring him right in the face! Several of the battle scars that marred the Volgarian's face seemed to pulse and throb. The hulking Volgarian was naked, his flaccid member flopping about as he moved.

"I knew I smelled something tasty," Raker snarled. Raker grabbed for Joktala's face with his fat, stubby fingers but the Takan quickly ducked away. Joktala backed into Rin, stumbling over his friend's legs, falling to the floor.

The Volgarian quickly followed them into the hallway. His voice rumbled from his throat. "You made a bad mistake coming here, Takans."

Rin recovered immediately, hurtling his dagger at the approaching brute, taking stumbling steps backwards as the hulking Volgarian approached.

The blade sunk into Raker's bare shoulder but did nothing to deter him. The Volgarian ignored the spurting blood that jetted out of the gash in his shoulder completely. "A very bad mistake." He stalked towards the Takans.

From his position on the ground, Joktala

grabbed one of the fallen arrows that had spilled from his quiver and jabbed it into the Volgarian's bare leg. The Volgarian did not even flinch or even seem to feel the arrow penetrating his flesh. He reached down and grabbed Joktala by the neck, lifting him up off the floor, viciously crunching his throat with a savage squeeze of his massive hand! Blood spurted from Joktala's mouth as he flopped wildly in the Volgarian's grip, the dark liquid splashing the walls.

Rin's face flooded with horror as the blood of his friend splattered across his cheeks and his nose. "Joktala!" He leaned against the hallway wall, still stumbling backwards, moving away from Raker, not really thinking, just knowing he was in grave peril.

Raker released his grip and Joktala dropped to the floor, the Takan's body flopping and his limbs twisting askew at odd angles as he struck the landing. The Volgarian turned to glare with burning eyes at Rin; his flaccid member was now partially erect and growing larger as he approached Rin. "Come to me and I kill you quick. Make me work and I kill you slow." His eyes were dark in the dim hallway, but they still seemed to glow with a deep malevolence, his hatred and contempt of Takans rising up from within him, burning its way out of his eyes.

Rin turned to run but another Volgarian was now standing at the other end of the hallway, blocking the exit. Rin saw a door to his left, grabbed at its knob and yanked the door open, fleeing inside.

Inside the room, Rin whipped the door shut

behind him and threw the bolt just as a large mass rammed into it from outside the room! He backed away quickly from the door, his eyes overflowing with terror. His chest felt tight, his breathing hoarse and ragged.

Raker's angry voice penetrated the wooden door. "You're going to die painfully now, Takan. Oh, how you're going to die."

Bam! Bam! Bam! Intense pounding rang out as fists slammed repeatedly into the door, filling Rin's ears with their threatening sound.

"Open the door, blueback scum," Raker growled from the other side of the door. Bam! Bam! Bam! His pounding fists growled out their own demand.

Rin continued backing away from the door, his eyes darting this way and that, looking for some way out. He bumped into something and a blue hand suddenly fell across his shoulder. He jerked away quickly and spun to see a naked Takan staring at him with yellow, vacant eyes. The dead Takan's skin was streaked with dirt, its face ravaged by insects and the savage bite of time.

Rin looked up to see another dead Takan lying naked atop the first Takan. And another dead Takan atop of that one. He twisted and turned, shutting his eyes tight, trying to get the horrible sight from his mind. But everywhere he turned in the room and opened his eyes he saw more dead Takans. Males and females were piled together, along with elderly Takans and younglings. Some of these Takans were unfortunate victims of the mulger stampede in the Falling Stream marketplace. There were dozens lying dead, stacked naked in piles like cords of wood, all coated with dirt and grime and smears of dried blood. Rin backed into a wall, struggling to catch his breath. The foul odor that filled the room finally assailed his nostrils and he fought back a choking gag.

Outside, the pounding on the door continued, but now the pounding sound was joined by the ominous sound of the wood beginning to crack. The threat in Raker's voice was clearly audible from the other side of the door. "Now you die slow."

Then Rin saw a face that made his heart freeze in his chest. He stepped closer to the body, wanting to make sure, hoping that he was wrong. But he was not. "What is going on here?" he muttered to himself, an obvious trembling fear in his words.

The wood cracked loudly behind him. The Volgarians were almost through.

Then, Rin glanced up and saw a window high up on the wall. It was too high to reach with outstretched arms and the ledge was too high to reach even with a surging jump. He would need help to reach it, a ladder of some sort, a crate, something. He looked about the area and saw that several dead Takan corpses were laid in a pile beneath the window. Rin clenched his jaw, knowing what he had to do.

He reached out and put a tentative hand on the arm of one of the nude corpses, struggling to avoid succumbing to the nauseous feeling welling up in his stomach as his fingers touched the cold, clammy flesh. He started to climb up the stack of dead bodies, doing his best to avoid stepping on anyone's face.

The door burst open behind him and Raker charged in, his face a snarling mask of absolute rage and hate. Two more big Volgarians were right on Raker's heels, charging into the room with him.

Rin turned away from the approaching Volgarians and scrambled up the pile of bodies, desperate to reach the top of the stack of dead flesh. He stood precariously balanced on the back of the face-down body at the top of the pile, then leaped for the window ledge. And missed. He slid back down the wall, landing atop the pile of Takan corpses. A few of the corpses made grotesque flatulent noises as his falling weight crushed down on them. The fetid odor already present in the room thickened to an even deeper stench.

Raker grabbed for him but Rin grabbed a corpse's leg and lashed out, whipping the still-attached appendage around, striking Raker in the face, using the leg like some hideous club, momentarily knocking Raker back into the other two Volgarians.

Rin scrambled to his feet and jumped again, this time grabbing the ledge successfully with the tips of his fingers. He pulled himself up on the ledge, moving quickly, his desperation fueling his strength, then immediately threw his shoulder against the glass without a second's hesitation. The window shattered, and the momentum of his thrust sent him tumbling into the night.

Rin hit the ground hard with a grunt, but quickly staggered to his feet and stumbled off away from the house, his fear propelling him on, the fresh air of the night filling him with renewed energy.

HAVENMORE TAVERN
A TAKAN TAVERN IN FALLING STREAM - NIGHT

Music filled the air, the notes seeming to swirl around the smoke that twisted and weaved in this modest establishment. A short bar lined the far left wall. Tables filled the middle of the room, their chairs filled with Takan patrons, some smoking, some drinking, some chewing sweet leaves, all of them staring at the entertainment taking place on the small stage at the far end of the room. This was the Havenmore Tavern, a Takan establishment.

On that stage, a Takan female danced a very sensual dance as she sang a haunting love song. Her name was Alaysia Grinto, of the Grinto Clan. Her clothes seemed to move across her body, revealing a smattering of skin here, a glimpse of forbidden flesh there, then covering her again completely. She was strikingly beautiful with jet black hair that fell past her shoulders, her voice hypnotic. Her yellow eyes sparkled with life and it was clear she loved what she was doing, reveling in the crowd, the attention, thriving on the emotion of her own performance.

Rin sat at one of the tables, trying to take a sip of a brew from a mug but his hand was shaking so badly that he could not. He set the mug back down on the table. He watched Alaysia sing for a moment, trying to force himself to be still, but he could not stop fidgeting in his seat. He curled his trembling fingers into fists, but then his hands started to shake. He thrust his arms down to his sides so he wouldn't have to see his shaking hands.

Alaysia finished her song, smiled at the whistles and claps and shouts for more, then turned to head to the back of the stage. Her dress shifted again just before she disappeared into the back of the tavern, giving everyone watching her a teasing glimpse of her perfectly rounded buttocks before she vanished into the shadows.

Rin got up from his seat and followed her, moving through the wildly cheering audience.

****

"It was him, Alaysia," Rin said. "I swear it. You have to believe me!"

Alaysia sat across from Rin at her dressing table, studying him with troubled eyes as he paced back and forth in the small dressing room. She was wearing a plain white robe that covered her body. "Your father was buried two moons ago, Rin. Unlike you, *I* was there. I saw them put him into the ground.

"You don't think I know that?" Rin's words came out hot and tight.

"So how could his body be there in some Volgarian house? Why would he be there?" She looked hard at Rin, her eyes narrowing slightly. "And what were you doing there?"

Rin hesitated. "It was supposed to be a Human

38

house. Joktala… we were…"

Alaysia looked sharply at Rin, suddenly uncomfortable but trying her best to mask her emotions. "Joktala? What was he doing there?"

"He… he was bringing me there to… he was trying to cheer me up… after you…" Rin looked away from her.

"And just where is that jreck?" Alaysia asked. She rose up to move to a nearby side table, grabbing a small jar of cosmetic cream.

Rin stopped pacing. He was quiet for a long moment. He slowly looked up at her, a clear look of anguish discoloring his face. "He's dead." He lowered his head.

Alaysia stared hard at Rin. "What?"

Rin looked back up at her. "The Volgarians killed him."

"He's dead?" Alaysia just looked at Rin with a flat expression, not able to comprehend, not wanting to comprehend what he had just told her.

Rin looked away from her and nodded, barely moving his head.

"You're pulling one of your stupid pranks on me, right?" She shook her head. "I'm really not in the mood." She put the jar of cream back down.

"I wish it was a prank. I really do," Rin said. "Volgarians killed him. I saw them do it."

Alaysia stood motionless, shock now overpowering her as the reality of Rin's horrifying news sunk in. She managed to stagger back to her chair and sat heavily. "Dead?" Her face tightened and her body tensed as a cold rage spread through her. "You've really done it this time, Rin. You just don't know when to quit, do you? First, the Humans wanted to put you on trial for selling the sweet leaf to their females. And then the PowderKeepers wanted to ban you from their shops for trying to pass fake coins on them—"

"I didn't know those were fake. Joktala told me they…" At the sound of his friend's name coming out of his mouth, Rin's voice died away.

Alaysia set her jaw tight. "And now the Volgarians probably want to kill you, too. Who are you going to try to antagonize next? The entire Takan Council?" Alaysia ran a brush angrily through her luxurious mane of black hair. She laughed a biting, bitter laugh. Then she abruptly whirled on Rin, her eyes flashing, and threw the brush at him, striking him square in the chest. "Why the hell are you here, Rin? I don't want your problems anymore! I just want to do my work and write my songs and lead a simple life. Is that too much to ask?" Alaysia's anger rose. "Is it?"

Rin absently rubbed his chest as he looked at her, then lowered his gaze. "I didn't know where else to go."

"You should go to the Council. A Volgarian murdering a Takan is pretty damn serious." Suddenly, Alaysia charged Rin, clawing at him with her sharp nails! "You bastard!"

Rin grabbed her wrists, keeping her nails away from his face as best he could. He shook her roughly, taking some of the fight out of her. "What's wrong with you?"

"Joktala's dead because of you!"

Rin frowned. "Since when did you…" Then, a

startling, painful realization hit Rin square in the face. "It was Joktala…" Rin let go of her quickly, as if her skin had suddenly become scalding to the touch. He took a few stumbling steps back, moving away from her.

Alaysia pointed to the door. "Get out!"

Rin stared at his former lover with shocked eyes. "Joktala… that Volgarian-loving fuck… he did it to me again." His muttered words were more for himself than for Alaysia. Suddenly, Rin threw his head back and laughed uproariously.

Alaysia stared at him as if he had lost his mind.

"Even when you're dead, you get the upper hand," Rin muttered, and then he laughed again. Finally, Rin's laughter subsided, but he made no move towards the door. He looked back to Alaysia, a solemn look filling his eyes.

Alaysia glared hotly back at him. "What? What more do you want? Haven't you done enough?"

Rin kept his gaze locked on hers. "I still need your help."

Alaysia raised her chin defiantly. "Elders curse you, Rin."

"I have to know about my father. I have to know for sure."

Alaysia scowled at him. "So go dig him up."

Rin stared hard at Alaysia.

She looked at him for a moment, then disbelief flooded into her face.

THE KINTOEL TAVERN – A HUMAN-OWNED
ESTABLISHMENT – NIGHT

Lizette entered the Kintoel Tavern, her face hidden by a hood. The stage in the middle of the room was empty, the performers between shifts. The patrons in the tavern were subdued, silently nursing drinks or quietly talking between puffs on their pipes. She moved to the bar and leaned up against the scarred wooden counter.

The barkeeper, Harris Drake, moved over to her. He was a thin Human male with a thick growth of brown beard covering his face. "What'll you have?"

"Answers," Lizette said.

Lizette glanced up at Drake, revealing her face to him.

Drake took a few stunned steps backwards, his face draining of color. He bumped into a shelf of bottles and one of the bottles fell, smashing against the floor. "I thought you were… gone." He made no move to clean up the shattered glass or mop up the spilled liquid contents that had been contained in the bottle.

Lizette scowled. "You don't seem happy to see me, Drake."

Drake sputtered, trying his best to cover his reaction. "Sure I am, Lizette. Sure I am." He reached down and picked up a few pieces of the broken bottle, dropping them into a nearby garbage pail. He glanced back over to Lizette. "How… how are you? You okay?"

Lizette cocked her head and looked at Drake earnestly. "Why wouldn't I be?"

"I don't know," Drake said. He made an awkward shrugging motion. "It's just that I heard about Noreena and you and those Volgarians a few days ago. I thought you were…"

Lizette leaned in closer to Drake. "You thought I was what?"

"D… dead," Drake stammered.

"You nervous about something, Drake?"

"N… n… no."

Lizette studied the barkeeper for a long, silent moment. "I got this funny feeling all of a sudden, Drake. It's kinda makin' my stomach turn." She paused. "Like you never expected to see me again. Now why is that, do you think? Maybe you know something about those Volgarians that tried to snatch me. Maybe you know where Noreena is."

TAKAN CEMETERY GROUNDS - NIGHT

Rin led Alaysia through the Takan cemetery to an area of land marked by numerous identically shaped tombstones. Each one was about three feet high, made of carved stone, rounded at the top. This was Rin's family plot. Around them, a soft wind bent the trees, whispering dark secrets as it moved through their gnarled branches. The two orange-hued moons in the sky illuminated the graveyard with a soft light, throwing slowly slithering shadows all about them as the trees swayed in the slight breeze. Rin stood at the foot of his father's grave, shovel in hand.

Alaysia stepped up next to him, the light from the torch she held washing over the grave. At first glance, the gravesite looked completely undisturbed. "After you dig up your father's bones, you'd better go straight to the Council," Alaysia said.

Rin nodded. "That's the deal, isn't it?"

"Your deal. If I didn't know you were as stubborn and as dimwitted as a drunk Human, I would never have agreed to this. This is stupid, Rin." She shook her head. "No, *I'm* stupid for coming with you."

Rin looked at her. "You owe me."

Alaysia frowned. "I don't owe you anything."

"Then why are you here?"

Alaysia gave him an annoyed glare. "Just shut up and dig."

Rin did not want to shut up nor let it go. "You're the one who left me."

The incredulous look on Alaysia's face was genuine. "I left you? You're the one who kept running out on me."

Rin shook his head, the movement slight, his head barely moving back and forth. "I never ran out on you."

Alaysia frowned. "Rin, I'm not going to argue with you. I want someone to be there when I need them. You never were. Always going off looking for something you're never going to find."

"Alaysia, I—"

Alaysia interrupted him. "Rin, you don't need

to find yourself. You're right here."

Rin scowled at her and turned to look over at his father's tombstone. His father's name was etched into the stone, and that's all. Kenko Grinto. No dates, no words. Just his name, following the Grinto Clan tradition of simple burials and simple monuments. Rin thought about his father, a few memories of the good times they had flashing through his head. Images of them hunting together, cooking together, the first time he took Rin to one of the taverns to watch the singers, all played across his mind. They were good memories, pleasant memories. He felt the sadness of his father's loss starting to well up inside him, but he knew he didn't have time to let that emotion overtake him now.

He stared down at the gravesite, finally really taking it all in. The mound of dirt covering the main portion of the grave seemed odd, almost sunken. It should have had a slightly rounded raised mound to it, but instead the dirt seemed to form a slight concave hollow. It looked different from the last time when he had visited his father's grave. "Just keep watch. Something's not right." He started to dig.

THE KINTOEL TAVERN – A HUMAN-OWNED
ESTABLISHMENT – NIGHT

Drake poured Lizette a drink and set it down in front of her. "Here, drink this. It'll... calm your stomach."

Lizette glanced at the mug, staring at the reddish-yellow liquid within, then slowly shifted her gaze back to Drake. "*You* drink it."

Drake shook his head. "I'm working."

"You drink it." She put more force behind her words, and her repeated request came out as more of a demand than a suggestion.

Drake tried to shrug, but again the motion came off forced and it looked more like a disturbing twitch. "Hey, if you don't want it, then don't drink it." Drake took the glass away from her and dumped the drink into a nearby sink. The liquid foamed and bubbled ominously.

A heavily drunken Volgarian sitting at a nearby table belched a volcanic belch. The other Volgarians sitting nearby roared with approval. The belching Volgarian staggered to his feet, grabbed at his crotch area, unleashed his member from his breeches, and began urinating in a large pisspot situated near the table. His stream missed the pisspot most of the time, the liquid splashing off the rim or just hitting the wooden floor outright to create small puddles of Volgarian urine.

Drake scowled at the sight and yelled at the Volgarian. "Hey, I just cleaned that floor!"

The drunken Volgarian turned to look at Drake, spraying his urine across several Human males sitting at a nearby table as his body turned along with his head.

"Hey, you stupid Volgarian fuck!" one of the Human males shouted, angrily wiping at the urine dripping down his cheek.

Two of the Human males rose and shoved the

drunken Volgarian, each pushing hard against one of his shoulders, knocking the heavily intoxicated drunk to the floor.

In a matter of moments, the tavern erupted into a free-for-all, with Humans swinging at Volgarians with clenched fists, and Volgarians pounding Humans back with their clubbed fists.

Two Human female performers dressed in sheer outfits who had just stepped onto the stage quickly rushed backstage.

"Take it outside!" Drake yelled at the brawling patrons.

A blue flash of light blinded Drake for a moment and he blinked quickly to clear his eyes. When his vision cleared, he saw Lizette standing next to him on the same side of the counter, holding a shimmering blue blade near his throat with a gloved hand.

"Talk motherfucker," Lizette snarled.

Visible behind Lizette, the brawl continued unabated. A Human male grabbed a chair and cracked it over the head of a Volgarian; one of the wooden legs on the chair shattered, sending shards of wood spraying everywhere.

"Aww damn, come on Lizette, they're wrecking my place," Drake said, unable to keep the whining tone out of his voice.

Lizette shifted the blazing blue blade closer to Drake's neck. "And I'm gonna wreck you if you don't tell me what they did with Noreena."

Drake responded immediately, making no effort to protest or deny knowledge of the situation. "Alexian bought you. He gave you to the

Volgarians."

Lizette's scowl deepened. "He bought me? How the fuck can somebody buy me?"

"I sold your performer contract to him," Drake said. He dipped his chin and looked down, trying to get a better glimpse of the glowing blue blade that was sending intense waves of icy coldness over his neck.

"You sold me to Alexian?" Lizette showed Drake a grim smile. She turned her wrist quickly and shoved the tip of the ice blade into Drake's throat, then pushed it in deeper. The skin in his neck stiffened, freezing any blood that might have escaped from the wound. Then his face grew rigid, his flesh solidifying into a hardened shell of ice. Within seconds, his entire upper body had frozen solid. "Guess what?" Lizette made a fist and slammed it into Drake's face. His head and shoulders shattered into a million pieces of icy fragments that twinkled and sparkled as they spun and twirled towards the floor. "He's gonna want a refund."

TAKAN CEMETERY GROUNDS - NIGHT

Rin was now deeper into the grave, nearly up to his waist. A pile of dirt near the gravesite grew larger with each shovelful of earth that he threw atop it. "It's not here."

Alaysia frowned. "What?" She shifted the torch to better illuminate where Rin was digging. He was a good three feet down into the ground now.

"His coffin," Rin said. "It's not here. I should have reached it by now." With growing urgency, Rin dug harder, thrusting the shovel deeper. "It's not here."

Thunk. His shovel hit something that sounded like wood being struck.

"I think you found it."

Rin frowned up at Alaysia, then returned to digging, more frantic and furious than ever. He still could not rid himself of the notion that something was wrong. Something was very wrong. He tossed the shovel down near the side of the grave and bent down into the hole to brush away more of the dirt with his hands. After a few swipes, he paused and rose back up. He found himself staring down at what appeared to be numerous rows of wooden boards, not the singular flat piece of a coffin lid that he had expected to see. He paused for a moment, resting almost waist deep in the hole. He reached for the shovel on the side of the grave and gripped the handle.

Crack! Suddenly, the boards split, the wood splintering under his weight. Rin dropped into the ground, grasping futilely for a hold in the dirt but the shovel in his hand prevented him from getting any kind of solid grip. He disappeared beneath the earth!

"Rin!" Alaysia leaned over the grave to peer urgently into the hole, her eyes wide. "Rin!" She raised the torch and moved it around, trying to illuminate the interior of the hole as best she could. "Rin!"

There was silence for a long moment, then Rin responded from below. "I'm okay. I'm okay."

More silence.

Then Rin's voice again filtered up from the gaping hole in the earth. "I think I'm in some kind of... Alaysia, you need to come down here."

*****

Rin held Alaysia by the waist as she lowered herself into the hole. "He's gone," Rin said. "My father's body is not here." Rin picked the burning torch up off the ground and the torchlight revealed that they were in a narrow tunnel that branched off into various side tunnels a few dozen feet from where they stood. The shovel lay nearby on the damp ground of the tunnel floor.

Alaysia wasn't listening to him, her attention focused on their odd surroundings. "What is this place?"

Rin moved down the tunnel a few feet, raising the flame to reveal a similar set of wooden boards propping up the earth above them, the planks similar to those that he had cracked and fallen through in his father's grave. He moved down a few feet and saw another set of wooden boards. He moved again and saw another. He darted into a side tunnel.

Alaysia called out after him in a hushed, but urgent whisper. "Rin, wait!" Alaysia chased after him, finding him standing below yet another set of wooden boards.

"They're taking them all." Rin stood

motionless, his entire body tensing, every muscle in him growing taut as the reality of what he was seeing overwhelmed him.

"Let's get out of here," Alaysia said.

Rin nodded, but did not move. "They're taking them all."

A sudden alarm flared up in Alaysia's face and she hissed an urgent warning. "I hear someone!"

Rin lifted his head, hearing it as well. Voices! He shoved the torch into the ground, rolling it in the dirt, dousing the flames. Everything went black. Only a faint column of pale orange light cast by the twin moons streaming into the hole in his father's grave was visible in the near distance. "By the Elders, the shovel! It's back by the grave."

The voices grew louder. Rin glanced into the wider main tunnel area and saw a circle of light approaching, the light growing brighter. He pulled back quickly. "Volgarians," he whispered.

Alaysia kept her voice low. "Here? That's not possible."

Rin and Alaysia backed deeper into the side tunnel, keeping their gazes focused on the main tunnel as they moved backwards. They huddled in the darkness as a group of Volgarians passed by, one of them carrying a Takan corpse over his wide shoulders. The Volgarians were streaked with dirt; two of them carried massive shovels, while several others carried planks of wood.

Rin scowled. Alaysia gripped nervously at his arm.

The last Volgarian in the line, a fat Volgarian clutching a hammer, paused for a moment at the entrance to the side tunnel where Rin and Alaysia were hiding. He raised his snout-like nose for a moment and sniffed the air. He looked straight into the tunnel, straining to see anything in the blackness, but it was far too dark for him to see anything. After a moment, he turned away and moved on, following his companions.

The sounds of the Volgarian footsteps and their voices faded into the distance.

Cautiously, Rin moved towards the main tunnel and peered in the direction the grave-robbing monsters went. The light in the distance faded into darkness.

Alaysia stepped up behind him. "What are they doing? What are Volgarians doing on Clan grounds?" Her questions came out in hushed whispers. "What have you gotten me into this time?"

Rin shushed her. "Let's just get out of here."

They moved as quickly as they could in the darkness of the tunnel, heading back to the area below his father's open grave. Moonlight shone down from above, the orange-hued light streaming in through the hole Rin had fallen through. Rin scanned the ground around him. "The shovel's gone." Rin nervously looked around the area, quickly scanning the ground again, but he did not see anything nearby except the broken planks of wood.

"Let's just get out of here," Alaysia urged, echoing his sentiment from a few moments earlier.

Rin lifted Alaysia up into the hole, holding her firmly around her waist. A whiff of her sweet scent brushed past his nose as he raised her up and he felt a sudden surge of sadness; he forced himself not to think of their past together and continued to help her climb out. She grabbed the edge of a cracked board and pulled herself up and out of the hole. Rin jumped up and grabbed the edge of the board.

Back up in the graveyard, Alaysia turned to help Rin out of the hole. She grabbed at his shoulder and started pulling him up, but she got in his way more than she helped him.

"Move, move!" Rin shouted at her. "Move out of the way."

Alaysia frowned and stepped back. "I was just trying to help you, you jreck!"

Suddenly, Rin was quickly, violently pulled back into the grave! His head slammed into one of the cracked wood planks, the force of the blow dazing him.

"Rin!" Alaysia shouted in alarm.

Rin struggled feebly to get out of the grave, his fingers clutching weakly at the cracked board as he struggled to pull himself up out of the hole.

Alaysia grabbed his arms and pulled. Slam! Again, Rin was pulled sharply downwards. The force of the pull dragged Alaysia down to her knees and she lost her grip on Rin. "Rin!"

Rin disappeared into the blackness of his father's grave, leaving Alaysia standing alone in the desolate cemetery. "Rin!" Alaysia cried out Rin's name again and again. She put her face near the grave opening and a spear tip shot out of the darkness, missing her face by an inch! Alaysia rocketed to her feet.

"We'll find you, Takan!" a Volgarian threatened from the dark hole.

The deadly tip of the spear descended back into the hole, then abruptly jutted back up again, seeking its prey.

Alaysia's face filled with true terror and she spun away from the grave to flee into the night.

The Volgarian threat followed her into the darkness. "We'll find you!"

HOME OF HUMAN JASON ALEXIAN - NIGHT

Lizette crouched behind a row of bushes, watching Jason Alexian rant and rave at several Volgarians, Raker among them. Alexian was a tall, burly Human male with a thick growth of red hair and beard. Lizette could not hear what he was saying, but he was obviously pissed off from the nature of his wildly gyrating arms. He paced back and forth just outside the front door of his house, stopping to yell at one Volgarian or another at sporadic intervals, then continuing to pace. He finished his ranting and went inside the house. The Volgarians headed off away from the house.

Lizette waited until the Volgarians had disappeared into the distance, then moved closer to the house, reaching a side door. She inched along the wall and peered inside a window to see—

—Alexian kissing a Takan female, who was lying prone on a couch. But the Takan wasn't responding; she wasn't kissing Alexian back, nor was she fending off his advances in protest. From what Lizette could see, the Takan appeared dead. Her chest beneath her buttoned-up tunic did not move, nor did she have any motion in her fingers, not even a twitch.

Alexian caressed the Takan's face, stroking her cheeks with the backs of his fingers. He moved a lock of her hair away from her face, tucking it around her pointed ear. He inserted a finger into her mouth, rubbing it around her lips, then drawing it back out. Then Alexian started undressing the Takan, moving slowly with the top buttons, obviously savoring the moment as he revealed her blue-skinned breasts to his lust-fueled gaze.

"Alexian, you are one sick fucker," Lizette muttered. She moved along the wall and reached another window. She tried to raise the window but it was locked.

HOME OF TAKAN ALAYSIA GRINTO - NIGHT

Alaysia sat at her kitchen table, obviously still very disturbed over the night's events. Her hands and face were smeared with dirt, her dress streaked with mud. She tried to take a drink but her hand was shaking so badly she could barely raise the mug. She got up and headed for the door, muttering to herself. "The Council has to know…"

She reached for the door when suddenly a heavy pounding rang out from the opposite side of the door, freezing her in her tracks. She quickly lowered her hand and backed away from the door, her eyes filling with fear. Volgarians. Alaysia moved back deeper into the kitchen. She didn't think they would find her so quickly.

The pounding sound rang out again.

Outside, something crossed in front of her back window, throwing a moon-lit shadow over her. They had her house surrounded!

Alaysia froze for a moment, then quickly whirled towards the floor-length window that led to her backyard. She grabbed a long, serrated-edged knife from the counter and went to the window, looking out to see—

—nothing. Only softly swaying trees moved outside in the night. Then, a bird flew past, startling her, throwing another moon-lit shadow over her. Alaysia bit back a scream and re-gripped the knife tightly. She stared out the window for a long moment, then cocked her head, listening.

Alaysia turned back to look at the front door. The pounding sound had now stopped, the room falling into silence. She could hear her own scared breath filling her ears. She re-gripped the knife, making sure she had a firm hold on the handle of the blade.

Crash! The back window exploded open as a dark shape came hurtling through it! Alaysia was knocked to the floor by the lunging shape, her knife jarred loose from her grip despite the firm hold she had on the weapon. But she quickly recovered and grabbed the dropped blade, sinking it deep into her attacker as the shadowed form of the dark shape loomed over her.

The attacker grunted and fell to the floor, dropping into a shaft of moonlight, the blade sunk deep in the attacker's chest, the handle jutting out.

Alaysia hurried back to her feet and stared down with wide, horrified eyes. "Joktala!"

A ragged, bloody piece of cloth encircled Joktala's throat. He clutched feebly at the blade sunk into his chest where Alaysia had just stabbed him.

"Joktala. Elders curse my soul!" She quickly corrected herself. "No, Elders curse *your* soul. Rin said you were dead!" Alaysia dropped to her knees beside him and hugged him desperately, kissing him wildly all over, pressing her lips to his forehead, to his cheeks, to his lips. "Oh, Joktala. I thought I'd never see you again!"

Joktala pushed her away with all the feeble strength he could muster.

"What? What's wrong?" Alaysia asked. Her face took on a hurt, crestfallen expression, Joktala's rejection of her affection distressing her greatly.

He again clutched weakly at the blade in his chest, pressing his fingers down on the area of his flesh surrounding the blade, as if trying to block more blood from seeping out of him.

Alaysia's eyes went wide, as if she had just seen the weapon embedded in his body for the first time. "By the Elders!" She grabbed the knife's handle and began easing it out of his chest. Blood oozed out of the wound as she pulled on the blade.

Joktala scrunched up his face in pain as she removed the bloodied blade from him, the noises coming out of him sounding like harsh nasal grunts.

Alaysia quickly cut off a piece of her dress with the knife and pressed it hard against Joktala's wound. Joktala tried to speak, but the words would not come. Alaysia saw his lips moving and moved closer to him. "What? What is it?" Alaysia squinted at him, confused.

Joktala reached up and grabbed her hair, forcing her to look at his lips as he struggled to raise his head off the floor. He mouthed the word "leaf."

"Leaf?" Alaysia asked.

Joktala gritted his teeth, nodding harshly. He coughed violently, releasing his grip on her as he lowered his head back down to the floor.

Alaysia had to think for a moment, then understood what he was trying to tell her. "Okay. I'll get some. I've got some healing gel, too." She rose to her feet, moving out of the kitchen.

Joktala closed his eyes.

Alaysia quickly returned with some sweet leaf and a healing gel. She put a piece of the leaf into Joktala's mouth. He chewed desperately and swallowed, grimacing with intense pain as the sweet leaf juices moved down his damaged throat. He made a motion with his fingers for another one and Alaysia obliged, handing him a second leaf. He devoured the second leaf as quickly as the first, wincing mightily again as he swallowed.

Alaysia spread some healing gel on the knife wound in his chest. The blood oozing from the cut coagulated quickly with the help of the healing gel, sealing the wound. "Was that you knocking on the door?" Alaysia asked as she continued to smear more healing gel around his chest wound.

Joktala nodded.

"I'm sorry. I thought it was the Volgarians coming after me."

Joktala turned his head slightly to look up at Alaysia, a deep frown crossing his brow.

HOME OF HUMAN JASON ALEXIAN - NIGHT

Lizette cut a hole in a window, melting her way in through the glass with her fire blade, the leather glove she was wearing protecting her hand from the heat of the blade's handle. She finished carving out an opening big enough for her to fit through, and then looked at the burning, red-hot blade in her hands. She did not quite know what to do with the flaming weapon so she kept it with her as she climbed inside the house, careful to keep the fire blade away from her skin and clothes as she crawled through the window.

Lizette moved through the room, quickly seeing that it was a study of some sort. A large overstuffed chair was positioned in one corner of the room. Two of the walls were lined with books, the rows of the leather-bound tomes reaching from floor to ceiling. The fire blade continued to glow hotly, casting her in an orangish-red glow wherever she moved, the light clearly giving her away, but she could not bring herself to part with it.

She moved to a large table in the center of the room, on which was a miniature diorama of a large compound ringed by coal black trees and flanked by a scale replica of the Crystal Falls. She moved closer to the table, eyeing the diorama, studying the detailed layout of buildings contained within the fenced compound. There were several structures of identical shape and size that could be living quarters or barracks on one side of the diorama. It reminded her of a prison camp of some kind, surrounded by a high fence. Guard posts were positioned along the fence at regular intervals. And the entire compound was framed by black-trunked trees, as if this place was going to be built deep within some wooded area. She felt a chill cooling her blood. Deep inside some Black Woods. A strange, oval object at the rear of the compound layout caught her eye. There was a much larger building positioned near this oval object.

Lizette walked along the side of the table, stopping before the odd oval shape near the large structure. It looked like a replica of a rainbow swirl of light, a whirlpool of bright colors. "A Worzon hole?" Lizette muttered. "What the hell are they building?"

Lizette leaned over the table to get a better look at the Worzon hole miniature when the tip of the fire blade hit one of the model buildings. The model quickly ignited and the flames spread rapidly across the table's surface.

Lizette stepped back quickly, fear flashing across her face. But then resolve quickly replaced her apprehension. She moved to a bookshelf and held the blade beneath a row of books. The books quickly caught fire. "Buy me will you, you corpse-fucking piece of shit." She grinned and moved around the room, setting fire to anything she thought would light.

HOME OF TAKAN ALAYSIA GRINTO - NIGHT

Joktala struggled to a sitting position and leaned back against the kitchen wall, grunting and groaning as he moved. His throat and chest wound were wrapped in clean bandages.

Alaysia sat on a chair nearby. She looked up from the writing scribbled on a piece of parchment in her hands. "You think the sweet leaf helped heal you?"

Joktala nodded. He scribbled some more words on another piece of parchment and handed it to Alaysia. Alaysia reached down and grabbed the parchment. She read it, then glanced over at him. "It's the only thing keeping you alive?"

Joktala grabbed the parchment from her, wrote some more, then handed it back to Alaysia. "Besides the new breathing hole in my chest, you mean?" Alaysia said, reading his words aloud. She looked over to Joktala with a soft expression. "I said I was sorry."

He motioned for more leaf, putting his fingers near his lips, making chewing motions with his mouth.

Alaysia shook her head. "I don't have any more."

Joktala motioned for the piece of parchment and Alaysia handed it back to him. He scribbled something and handed it back to her.

Alaysia read his words and looked back at him curiously. "You want to go to the PowderKeeper's now?"

Joktala nodded. He motioned for her to give him the parchment back. When she did, he scribbled a few more words and handed it back to Alaysia.

"They always have the strongest leaf," she said, reading back his words. She looked at him, eying his bandages, seeing the distress etched into his squinting eyes. "Can you even stand up?"

Joktala started to rise, but then dropped back down, wincing, clutching at the wound in his chest. He motioned for Alaysia to help him with a quick curling of his fingers. She set the parchment down on the table, put her arm around his shoulder and helped him to his feet. They stared at each other for a moment, then Alaysia kissed him sweetly, gently on the lips. "I'm so glad you're not dead," she said.

Joktala nodded in agreement and smiled. He winced and gingerly touched his throat. He hobbled to the table and wrote some more. He handed the parchment to Alaysia, his expression now dark and serious.

Alaysia shook her head. "No, Rin and I didn't find out what the Volgarians were doing with the bodies." She had told Joktala what had happened to her and Rin while she was bandaging him up earlier. Her face suddenly flushed hot with aggravation. "How am I supposed to go to work tomorrow? I need this job!"

Joktala wrote some more, his jaw set tight as he thrust the parchment at her.

"Well, good luck finding him because I'm going to the Council with this," Alaysia said. "They need to know what is going on." She tossed the parchment down to the table and crossed her arms beneath her breasts.

Joktala grabbed the parchment and wrote some more. He held the parchment up in front of her face.

Alaysia studied his words for a long moment, then looked over at him. "Yeah. That's what he said."

HOME OF HUMAN JASON ALEXIAN - NIGHT

Lizette reached the bottom of a set of stairs and moved into the dark basement. Upstairs, voices yelled as the fire in the study was being battled. Lizette glanced up, but really paid them no heed. It was too late to worry about that now. She had to find Noreena.

Lizette moved into a small corridor lined with what appeared to be holding cells of some sort, with a barred window set into each door. She peered into the first cell. It was unoccupied, nothing but an empty room with a hard-packed earthen floor.

She moved on, glancing into the second cell. "Noreena!"

Inside the cell, Noreena was naked, curled up in a ball in the far corner. A cot was positioned along the left wall, but Noreena had chosen to curl in the dirt near the opposite wall.

A roachrat, a furry, multi-legged rodent of sorts

about three inches long that was the product of a nightmarish marriage of a rat and a cockroach, was eating the food on a plate that rested on a tiny table near the cot. Another roachrat was sniffing at Noreena's ankles. This roachrat was bigger than its fellow picking away at Noreena's food, about five inches in length; it rose up on two of its six legs and waved its other four legs just inches above Noreena's exposed flesh, as if debating in its tiny brain whether to start feeding on this interesting source of meat now or not.

"Hey, beat it!" Lizette stuck the fire blade through the bars in the window, shaking it at the roachrat near Noreena's ankles. The insect beast turned its head to hiss defiantly at Lizette, but then scurried to join its partner at the food plate. "Noreena. It's me. It's Lizette! Wake up!"

Noreena did not stir.

Lizette tried the door, but a padlock kept it from opening. She put the fire blade to the shackle, pressing the hot blade against the metal loop on the lock. The metal began to redden, getting hot. The smell of molten metal filled the narrow corridor. "Hold on, baby. I'll get you out."

Voices yelled out in the distance, and they seemed to be drawing closer, getting louder. Lizette did her best to ignore them, but she could feel a tenseness tightening her shoulders. She was amazed she had gotten this far into the house without being seen, but she knew damn well that her luck was not going to last much longer. She glanced nervously over her shoulder, looking towards the stairwell where she had come into the basement, but there was no movement.

Finally, the melted lock fell to the floor with a soft clatter. Lizette again glanced nervously at the stairwell, uncertain how far the clanging sound of the falling lock had traveled, then quickly looked back to the cell door. She pulled on the door to open it, but quickly yanked her hand away from the metal. "Ow, that's fucking hot!" She ignored the burning pain in her hand and hurried into the cell.

Lizette moved to Noreena's side, dropping the still-burning fire blade to the earthen floor as she cradled her friend in her arms. A foul smell of urine and fecal stench assailed her nostrils but she ignored them. Noreena did not respond. Lizette tugged off her leather glove and touched her friend's face with both hands, caressing her with a growing desperation. "Noreena, it's me. It's Lizzie. You have to get up."

Noreena finally looked at Lizette, but there didn't seem to be any recognition in her eyes. She had a blank look to her stare.

"Come on. You have to get up. We have to get out of here right now." Lizette hauled Noreena to her feet, but Noreena's legs gave way and she fell back to the floor hard. Her arm landed on the fire blade and it immediately burned her flesh severely and singed the hairs on her arm. She cried out in pain, moving away from the fire blade, grabbing at her burn. The acrid smell of burnt hair and charred flesh immediately filled the room. Noreena's eyes finally seemed to focus on Lizette and recognition lit up her face. "Lizette, is that you? Is it really you?"

"It's me, baby. It's me." Lizette bent down to her friend. "You've got to get up. We've got to get out of here."

Noreena nodded and started to get up.

Suddenly, they heard footsteps quickly approaching. Voices. Very close. Lizette moved for the door and eased it shut. She motioned for Noreena to be still as she pressed herself against the wall near the cell window, staying out of sight of anyone who might look in.

"Takans are ugly slugs, ain't they?" A Volgarian said, his voice drawing closer.

"And they sure do stink," a second Volgarian said. "They always smell like flowers." A loud farting sound rang out from the hallway. "Did they find the other one yet?"

"No, but they will. Alexian won't be able to get stiff meat until they do. It's the only reason we're keeping this one alive. Alexian wants us to find out how much he knows."

"Cell four is empty. Throw him in there for now."

Suddenly, the footsteps and the voices stopped. Lizette's body tensed as she saw the fire blade still burning brightly on the dirt floor in the cell.

"What is this?" the first Volgarian asked, his voice just outside the cell door.

"The lock's been melted off!"

The footsteps drew closer, the footfalls quickening their pace.

"There's something burning in there! Watch him."

The cell door burst open and a Volgarian

charged into the room.

Lizette drew her last vial of ice powder from her pouch and shook it violently.

The Volgarian saw her movement and turned to her, quickly charging at her. Lizette hurled the vial at the Volgarian and it exploded against his shoulder, the powder smearing down along his arm. The Volgarian's arm quickly froze solid as a thick coating of snowy-white ice seeped over his flesh. Lizette rushed to him, grabbed his frozen arm and cracked it down over her knee, splintering it into a million fragments.

The Volgarian howled in pain and went down as blood spilled from his wound, steaming as it hit the coldness of what was left of his arm. Within seconds, his life faded, his body twitching in his death throes.

Lizette turned to see the second Volgarian right behind her, his sword raised and ready to strike her down! Suddenly, his abdomen burst into flames! He stood motionless for a moment, the sword still raised, and then he fell to his knees, screeching in pain, revealing—

—Noreena holding the fire blade in her hands behind him. She quickly dropped the blazing blade as the heat seared her hands.

Lizette spotted her dropped leather glove on the ground. She quickly donned the glove and immediately picked up the fire blade. She made quick work of the second Volgarian who was still howling in pain, slashing the crackling fire blade across his throat, drawing a deep groove of burnt, blackened flesh across his neck.

She grabbed Noreena's wrist and raced out of the room, pulling her along with her. They bolted out of the cell, running right into—

—a surprised Rin.

Lizette struck out immediately with the fire blade, but Rin managed to dodge the blow, and the swinging blade cut through air inches away from his stomach. "Hey, easy!" Rin exclaimed. "I'm not with them! I'm not with them! They brought me here!"

"Back off, Takan!" Lizette snarled. She waved the fire blade in front of her, the burning blade making trails of light in the air as she moved the blade quickly back and forth.

Noreena flattened her naked body against a nearby wall, terror again threatening to put her into a numbed stated of paralyzed fear.

Rin raised his bound hands, slowly backing away from the crackling weapon. He eyed the two Human females cautiously, stopping his gaze for a moment to look at the nude female trembling against the wall before putting his full attention back on the female wielding the fire blade. "Look, I want to get out of here just as bad as you."

Lizette eyed Rin's bonds warily. "You like to kill Volgarians?"

Rin's eyes narrowed. "I do now."

POWDERKEEPER SHOP
BORDERING HUMAN AND TAKAN
TERRITORY - NIGHT

Alaysia and Joktala cautiously entered the PowderKeeper's shop. "After this, we go to the Council," Alaysia said in a quick aside to Joktala as they moved towards the counter situated in the rear of the establishment.

Joktala nodded.

Around the shop, Gatherers chittered and flitted about, cleaning shelves, checking the contents of jars. Alaysia glanced around the shop, taking in all the myriad jars, fascinated by the sheer volume of different types of powders filling the clear containers. "Where do they get all these powders?" she asked Joktala, feeling the need to keep her voice low.

"I'm pretty sure they come from the Black Woods," Joktala said. He motioned to a few Gatherers working nearby. "They go in there and collect it."

The PowderKeeper, the same PowderKeeper Lizette had visited earlier, studied Joktala as he approached, looking curiously at the bandage around his throat, the blood stains on his tunic. "I know Takans heal fast," the PowderKeeper said as they stopped before the counter. "Takans strong. But you look like you seen war." The PowderKeeper moved one of his tendril fingers towards Joktala's mouth, probing at his lips. "You eat leaf. Keeper smell leaf. Leaf good. Leaf heal

69

inside. Leaf good for Takan."

Alaysia pointed to the two coins she had just dropped onto the counter. "Look, that's all we have."

The PowderKeeper glanced at the coins and made a soft whistling sound. Two Gatherers appeared, each grabbed a coin, and then disappeared back into the back room. Another Gatherer appeared from a different Gatherer-sized hole in the back wall and scampered up to the counter to lay something down on the counter before turning around and scampering back the way he had come.

The PowderKeeper pointed to the two tiny, shriveled sweet leaves on the counter that the Gatherer had just set down. "You give coin. I give leaf."

"But we need more than that," Alaysia said in protest, frowning at the paltry offering.

"Yes, leaf keep death away. Keeper sad for you. Keeper have no more."

Alaysia frowned. "You have no more leaf?"

The PowderKeeper waved his tentacles agitatedly in the air. "Keeper need leaf. Gatherers can't get leaf."

Joktala motioned for Alaysia to give him some parchment and a writing stick. She drew them from a pouch at her waist and handed them to Joktala. He wrote something and Alaysia read it aloud to the PowderKeeper. "Where is the leaf?"

The PowderKeeper studied Joktala. "Takan no voice talk?"

Alaysia shook her head slightly. "No. The

Volgarians crushed his throat."

The PowderKeeper's tentacles continued to move wildly about him, moving even more rapidly and jerkily as this news clearly agitated him greatly. "Keeper angry with Volgarians. Volgarians and Humans make monsters. Monsters kill Gatherers. Monsters steal leaf."

The PowderKeeper motioned to the Gatherers doing their duties within the shop, the small simian-like creatures continuing to dust shelves, clean out jars. "Humans try sell leaf to Keeper. Keeper no buy what he once gathered."

Joktala grabbed the parchment and wrote some more.

Alaysia glanced at the parchment, then looked up at the PowderKeeper. "What monsters?"

"Keeper show you." The PowderKeeper extended his tendrils from beneath his hair, moving them to both Joktala and Alaysia, making contact with the sides of their foreheads. The tips of the PowderKeeper's tendrils made a soft sucking sound as they adhered to the Takans' flesh. Then the PowderKeeper extended another tendril towards a nearby Gatherer, attaching it to the little creature's forehead.

Joktala and Alaysia both froze for a moment, then their eyes went wide.

BLACK WOODS
GATHERER'S MEMORIES

The PowderKeeper put Joktala and Alaysia into the mind of the Gatherer so they saw everything from low to the ground, as if looking through the eyes of the small creature.

Dark trees blanketed the landscape, their trunks as black as coal, their immensity staggering from the viewpoint of a Gatherer, towering far into the sky, their tops barely visible. The Gatherer moved through the dark trees, scampering along the ground, rustling through leaves, scurrying over fallen branches. He reached an area that opened up into an expanse of flat ground and paused behind the thick trunk of a coal-black tree to observe his surroundings. Before him, row upon row of sweet leaf plants covered the open ground beneath the trees, the plants growing as high as two feet. Workers tended to the plants, their race hard to discern fully in the darkness, but they were humanoid in shape, their bodies blanketed by black robes, their faces hidden within black hoods. Some of these workers carried rakes and they busily shifted the dirt in an empty patch of ground, as if preparing the land for additional planting. Other workers carried smaller tools they used to snip leaves off those sweet leaf plants that were ready for harvesting. Their hands looked oddly pale in the dim light, nearly white.

Other Gatherers appeared, moving towards the rows of sweet leaf plants. The little simian-like creatures began pulling the leaves off of the plants, putting them into the small leather pouches at their waists. This was their normal gathering routine and all the Gatherers chittered happily amongst themselves as they got to work. They seemed to pay no attention to the black-robed workers. And indeed they did not as the Gatherers had never encountered the likes of them before.

But that was a grave mistake as the black-robed workers quickly descended upon the Gatherers and began beating them to death with their tools! One black-robed worker plunged his spade straight into the throat of a Gatherer, violently splattering blood all over the nearby plant. Another Gatherer was impaled by the spikes of a rake and the black-robed worker raised up his rake to shake it viciously as the Gatherer squirmed and squealed in agony.

One of the Gatherers was struck hard in the shoulder by the end spike of a rake wielded by an attacking black-robed worker, but still managed to escape, twisting his way free of the spike, howling in pain as he fled through the dark trees.

More Gatherers squealed in terror as they were slaughtered. Many other Gatherers fled, escaping this unexpected assault from these black-robed workers they had never encountered before.

POWDERKEEPER SHOP
BORDERING HUMAN AND TAKAN
TERRITORY - NIGHT

The PowderKeeper released his tendrils from all three of them, the tendrils coming loose from Joktala's and Alaysia's foreheads with a slight sucking noise. "Those monsters." The PowderKeeper's body language was strange by Takan and Human standards, but there was an obvious deep sadness now visible within his expression, clearly noticeable by the limpness in his small mouth; the limpness of his tentacles also revealed some of his inner sadness as they drooped down at his sides.

Joktala and Alaysia remained quiet, still a bit overwhelmed by the images of what they had just experienced. The memories were strong and powerful, and almost felt as if they were now part of their own actual experiences.

The PowderKeeper's tentacles came back to life, weaving and dancing in the air. "Bring me leaf. I make strong powders for you." The PowderKeeper motioned to the Gatherers working in the shop, pointing several tentacles in their direction. "The Gatherers go. T'rok lead you."

One of the Gatherers on a nearby shelf stopped what he was doing and looked towards them. He lowered his tail, which he had been using as a duster, then leaped down onto the counter and moved closer to them. He was T'rok. An ugly scar marred his right shoulder; he was one of the

Gatherers who had fallen victim to the attacking black-robed workers. He looked at Joktala and Alaysia with imploring hazel eyes from within his rounded simian-face, as if he truly was desperate for them to let him accompany them. His fur had an orangish-brown color to it, sprinkled with rust-colored highlights, with a hint of white encircling his face. A small leather pouch was around his waist, positioned on the right side of his body, attached to a thin shoulder strap that he wore around his left shoulder and across his chest.

"I make strong weapons. Come. I show." The PowderKeeper motioned for Joktala and Alaysia to follow him into the back of the shop.

"Wait," Alaysia said.

The PowderKeeper turned back to face them.

Alaysia cocked her head quizzically at the PowderKeeper. "You want us to go into some Black Woods to bring you back some sweet leaf?"

"Yes. Heal throat. Make good as new. Keep Takan from death." The PowderKeeper paused to look at Joktala. "Death not good for Takan."

Joktala and Alaysia exchanged nervous glances.

HOME OF HUMAN JASON ALEXIAN - NIGHT

Lizette, a weak and trembling naked Noreena, and Rin moved cautiously down a hallway in Jason Alexia's home, looking for a way out. Noreena nursed her burned hand, gently clutching at her wrist.

"What the hell they grab you for Takan?" Lizette asked. "Did you piss on some Volgarians?"

"I saw Volgarians stealing Takan bodies from our graves," Rin said. "And then the Volgarians saw me."

"Volgarians stealing Takan bodies?" Lizette frowned. "For what?" And then she remembered what she had seen Jason Alexian doing with the dead Takan female, but she kept this to herself. There was no point in getting this Takan all riled up. Not now. They needed to get out of there first.

Rin frowned back at her, his jaw tightening. "That's what I'm going to find out."

Noreena stumbled and Rin caught her, holding her up by her elbow. Lizette glared at Rin, but then saw that Noreena needed to lean on someone to walk and her anger softened.

Rin motioned at Noreena with a tilt of his head. "Hold her." He nudged Noreena towards Lizette.

Lizette frowned at Rin, but let Noreena lean on her. "Thanks for helping."

Rin ignored her sarcastic remark. He removed his tunic and wrapped it around Noreena's shaking shoulders, then motioned for Lizette to let Noreena lean on him again.

Lizette looked sheepish. She shifted Noreena, helping her lift her arm around Rin's neck so she could lean on him.

Rin motioned to the fire blade that Lizette still clutched. "Can't you put that damn thing out?"

Lizette glanced at the blade burning in her gloved hand. "It has to run out of juice or something."

"Well, get rid of it. The light's going to give us away." Rin continued forward, easing Noreena onward along with him as he moved.

Lizette ignored Rin's demand and continued on down the hallway. She couldn't help but marvel at the muscular, smooth sleekness of Rin's naked upper body as he walked before her.

The three of them reached a large set of double doors and Rin stopped to peer through the window. His eyes went wide, then narrowed with rage.

*****

The double doors exploded open as Rin burst into the room! His face filled with outrage as he moved through this large, cavernous room. Table after table were lined up in neat rows throughout the room, each one holding what were clearly dead Takans. Various pieces of equipment were stationed on small stands near the tables, the stands filled with large glass tubes, flasks, beakers, and vials filled with all manners of liquids. Body parts floated in large trays on some of the stands.

Rin stopped before one of the Takan bodies and saw that part of the Takan's skull had been cut open and part of his brain had been sliced off. His eyes narrowed with an icy rage as he stared at a face he's known all his life, a face he saw days earlier stacked atop other Takan corpses in a room upstairs. "Father…"

"What the hell are they doing?" Lizette asked as she moved up to Rin. Noreena was leaning on her now, shuffling along with Lizette as best she could. Lizette stared at a Takan corpse, then looked over to Rin. "I saw Alexian about to hump one, but this—"

And then Rin went berserk, moving towards other tables in the room, swiping his arm across one of the equipment-filled stands, spilling its contents to the floor! He upended a stand with a violent outburst, gripping the edges of the stand and flipping his arms sharply upwards, sending more glass beakers shattering to the floor, spilling more liquid all about them. He broke more equipment, jars, vials; anything he could destroy, he did. The sounds of crashing tables and exploding glass echoed in the large room.

"Well, at least that's not going to give us away," Lizette muttered sarcastically.

The only thing Rin left untouched near him in his rampage was his father's corpse, the table his father's body was laying on, and a small side table filled with instruments that was near his father.

Suddenly, from around a corner, three Scitites came racing into the room. The Scitites were humanoid in shape, reaching five or six feet in height, resembling dark-skinned Humans with large eyes and thin, hairless bodies. Their heads were devoid of hair, their faces long, their small ears tight to their skulls, their chins rounded. They all wore identical tight-fitting, long-sleeved white shirts and white pants. The two Scitite males and one Scitite female moved quickly towards Rin.

"Scitites. I thought they never left their city," Lizette said to no one in particular.

"Stop! Stop!" one of the Scitite males shouted. "What are you doing?" His voice was shrill and scratchy, full of panic.

Rin turned to the approaching Scitites and they immediately saw that he was a Takan. All three Scitites froze for a moment. One of the Scitite males suddenly turned away and began racing back towards the hallway they had come from.

Rin moved fast, grabbing a scalpel from a nearby tray of surgical instruments that was on the stand near his father's table. He whipped it at the fleeing male Scitite, striking him in the neck. The Scitite stumbled and slammed hard into a wall, then fell to the ground to lay still.

Rin was on the fallen Scitite instantly, pulling the scalpel from his neck and slicing his throat with it. He stood and turned to face the other two Scitites, his breathing hot and ragged. Blood dripped from his fingers and slid down the blade of the scalpel as he raised it to point at the two remaining Scitites. "You tell me what you are doing with these bodies! What are you doing to my father?"

The remaining two Scitites could only stare in horror at the savage eyes of the Takan standing before them, both of them too scared to talk.

Lizette and Noreena could only stare in shock at the brutality displayed by their new companion.

Rin took a step towards the Scitites. Suddenly, he lurched forward, stabbing the female in the gut. She went down, gasping, clutching at her bleeding belly. Rin turned hot eyes to the remaining Scitite male, his yellow eyes gleaming with a fierce intensity. "Tell me now!"

The Scitite male stared with total dread at his fallen companion. His big eyes grew even wider. His body visibly trembled as he looked back at Rin.

Rin sliced the Scitite male's cheek, cutting at his flesh with a quick flick of his wrist. "Last warning," Rin said.

The Scitite grabbed at his cut face, stifling a cry, trying desperately to stop the flow of blood that was trickling down his fingers. "They're for the Volgarians! It's all for the Volgarians!" The Scitite male stared with growing dismay at the stabbed female as she groaned and curled herself into a ball, still clutching at her bleeding stomach. Rin stood between him and his fallen companion so he could not reach her. The Scitite male turned hot eyes to Rin, his pain and fear fueling his own anger. "We're trying to help you, damn you!"

"The Volgarians? What's for the Volgarians?" Rin's tone demanded an answer, as did the scalpel that he raised up towards the Scitite.

"The bodies!" the Scitite male said, his voice nearly a shriek. "They want Takan bodies. When you die—"

Rin took a threatening step closer to the Scitite male, glaring at him, pointing the tip of the bloody scalpel directly at him, his action cutting off the Scitite's words. "I'm not going to die."

The Scitite swallowed nervously. "Okay. When you..." he paused to quickly correct himself. "When a Takan dies, his brain changes. It secretes a chemical into your... into Takan blood that the Volgarians want. They need it for the Creator."

"Takan blood?" Rin said, repeating the Scitite's words as a question. "That's why they're stealing our dead?" Rin asked. "For our blood?"

The Scitite nodded, involuntarily licking away the blood that was sliding down from the cut on his cheek to his lips. "We are trying to recreate that chemical, recreate the… food the Volgarian Creator needs. Once we do, there's no need for—"

"You stupid Takan bastard…" The stabbed Scitite female looked up at Rin, still clutching her stomach, groaning as blood spilled forth from between her fingers. She gasped in pain, her large eyes squinting with the agony coursing through her. "It's either take a few of the dead bodies now and work on them, recreate what the Volgarians need, or soon the Volgarians will start harvesting living Takans like cattle. They've already been staging accidents in the Takan villages because they've emptied your graveyards." The Scitite female began coughing violently, clutching at her gashed stomach.

"Let us do our work," the Scitite male said. "We convinced the Volgarians to at least let us try. We want to stop the killing."

Rin was silent for a long moment, shaken by the news, trying to absorb the immensity of what the Scitites were telling him. But then he quickly recovered as a steely resolve came over his features. "My father will not be part of your work. Nor will any other Takan's father or mother or Clan brother."

The Scitite could read volumes in the silent look of determination that crossed Rin's features.

"You can't stop them all."

"Maybe not," Rin said. "But I'm going to start with you." Rin raised the bloody scalpel.

"Wait!" Lizette shouted.

The scalpel descended as Lizette's cry went unheeded.

DIRT ROAD NEAR FALLING STREAM - NIGHT

Alaysia was in the driver's seat of a small covered wagon being pulled by two mulgers. The dirt road was deserted at this late hour, the night illuminated by the pale orange light of the two moons; Fierbal loomed larger and brighter than its sister moon Dewlight, with Fierbal's brighter orange glow overpowering Dewlight's pale orange shine. Seven Gatherers raced along the road nearby as T'rok led the way, the little creatures easily keeping pace with the mulgers with their four-legged loping strides.

Inside the wagon, Joktala sat on a white pillow with frayed tasseled edges, staring absently into the night out of the open back flap. Various piles of items were clustered about the floor of the wagon, their contents hidden in shadows. He grimaced and touched his bandaged neck. He pulled a shriveled sweet leaf from the pouch at his waist and stared at it. He wanted so badly to use it, but he put the leaf back into the pouch. He only had one leaf left and he needed to preserve it for a time when the pain reached intolerable levels. He pulled the back flap closed, then turned to face the front of the wagon. He rose up and moved out of the covered area through a curtain, joining Alaysia, sitting next to her on the driver's bench, clutching at the healing wound in his chest as he sat.

Suddenly, the Gatherers started chattering loudly, dancing in place, not moving any further. They screeched at Joktala and Alaysia, indicating a row of black trees in the near distance, pointing directly at a cluster of Black Woods.

Joktala motioned for Alaysia to stop the mulgers and hurried out of the wagon, wincing with the sudden and sharp movement. He moved to T'rok and reached down to sharply tug on his orangish-brown fur, pulling the little creature roughly around to face him. Joktala held out his final sweet leaf to T'rok, pointing to the shriveled piece of green plant, then at the Black Woods.

The Gatherer scowled at Joktala, then took the leaf from him and put it into his little pouch at his waist.

Joktala waited for a moment, expecting something to happen, but the Gatherer just stared up at him with wide eyes. He motioned for the Gatherer to give him the leaf back, but T'rok did not acquiesce to his demand. Joktala then tried to pull T'rok's fingers away from where they were guarding his pouch. T'rok refused to open his pouch, turning his little shoulder away from the groping Takan. Joktala glared at him, motioning angrily at the pouch. His face scrunched up in pain and he gently rubbed at his aching throat.

Then, T'rok scampered away, moving to join

the other Gatherers. He showed his brothers what was inside his pouch and they whooped with glee, patting the little Gatherer on his back, chattering happily.

Joktala picked up a rock and was about to throw it at T'rok when Alaysia put her hand around his, stopping him. "I don't think that's a good idea," she said. "Especially since they're carrying all the powders the Keeper gave us." Alaysia gently pushed his arm back down to his side.

Joktala scowled, then uncurled his fingers and let the rock drop to the ground.

"Just wait here," she said.

Joktala watched as Alaysia walked over to the Gatherers and affectionately stroked their fur as she talked to them. He could see her lips move but from this distance he could not hear what she said. She gently stroked T'rok's fur on his head, then playfully scratched at a spot under his neck. The Gatherer loved the attention and raised his head so Alaysia could reach even more spots under his neck. She pointed at T'rok's pouch. All of the Gatherers pointed into the Black Woods and jumped up and down excitedly. Alaysia patted T'rok on the head, pointing at his pouch again. He gave up the leaf to her without hesitation.

Alaysia returned to Joktala and handed him the leaf. He immediately popped it into his mouth.

"You have to treat them with a little respect, Joktala, if you want them to do what you ask," Alaysia said.

Joktala closed his eyes for a moment as the sweet leaf deadened his pain.

"This is the place all right." Alaysia glanced at the Black Woods nearby. "This is near where T'rok was attacked by those monsters. This is where we'll find the leaf."

Joktala opened his eyes and nodded. He moved to the back of the wagon, throwing back the flap to reveal various piles of jagged-edged blades, throwing knifes heaped in mounds, and numerous other weapons and projectiles scattered about in the back of the wagon. It looked like they were ready for a small war. Joktala started piling some of the weapons into a bag.

"And then after this, we go to the Council," Alaysia said.

Joktala didn't even bother to nod.

HOME OF HUMAN JASON ALEXIAN - NIGHT

Lizette and Noreena moved cautiously down the hallway. Rin followed closely behind, struggling with the weight of his father's body that he was now cradling in his arms.

"I thought you bluebacks were always supposed to be kind and peaceful and fucking dignified. But hell, for a Takan you're pretty damn mean." Lizette paused. "Shit, I like that. I can't believe you wasted those Scitites like that."

"They chose the wrong allies," Rin said with a finality in his voice that made it obvious he no longer wanted to discuss it.

Lizette's fire blade crackled once, then went

out. Tiny wisps of smoke floated up off the metal. "Damn, it's dead."

Just then, Jason Alexian stepped into the corridor, flanked by two large Volgarians. "As you all will be soon," Alexian said. He pointed to the corpse of Rin's father. "I believe that belongs to me." Alexian was dressed in a red silken robe decorated in a flowery print, a sash tied about his waist keeping it closed.

Rin gritted his teeth as the two Volgarians took his father's corpse from him, but remained calm. The Volgarians were dressed in light armor that covered their chests and backs, as well as their arms. Their hands and heads were still exposed, devoid of any additional armor. They handled his father's body roughly, treating it like a sack of wheat; near where part of his father's skull had been sheared off, a bulging section of his brain matter threatened to drop out of the opening in his head. Fire burned in Rin's eyes. His hands clenched into fists at his sides. There wasn't much room in the tight confines of the hallway, not enough room to fight.

Lizette clenched her teeth, wanting to stick her knife in Alexian's gut with the consequences be damned, struggling to keep herself in check. "You fucking scumsucker. You fucking blueback humper. You fucking—"

Alexian smiled warmly at Lizette, holding his hand up, his action causing her to involuntarily bite off her words. "If I had known you were so courageous, Lizette, I would have kept you for myself," Alexian said. "My Volgarian friends told me you ran away like a roachrat running from the light and left your little friend all alone in the dark to fend for herself."

Lizette gripped her blade tighter. A slight hint of smoke drifted off the extinguished fire blade.

"I suggest you put that blade down," Alexian said to Lizette as he motioned to her weapon with a soft toss of his head. "You might hurt yourself."

Lizette curled her lip into a snarl. "I suggest you go fu—"

I know what you're doing," Rin said, blurting it out, interrupting Lizette as he stared hard at Alexian. "You won't get away with it."

Alexian laughed, quickly turning away from Lizette to look at Rin. "I've been getting away with it for the last twenty years, you stupid ass blueback. My only mistake was moving into this damn house six moons ago. I've had nothing but headaches ever since. Had I known it was an old pleasure house, I would never have bought it. The Volgarians convinced me to keep it running." Alexian pulled on his sash, tightening it. "Bad idea."

Rin could not hide the shock from his voice. "Twenty years…" His voice trailed off for a moment. "You've been stealing Takan bodies for twenty years?"

Alexian frowned. "Stealing?" He shook his head. "I'm no grave robber, blueback. Your Takan Council set this all up decades ago. They made a deal with the Volgarians to prevent them from attacking you." He paused and made a mournful face full of mock sadness. "Sadly, their supply is just about depleted. We were working on a new solution with the Scitites, but you took care of that with a few slit throats."

One of the Volgarian guards finally spoke, unable to contain himself. "After Ashenwall is built, there won't be any free Takans left."

Alexian glared at the Volgarian. That was not news to share. "Enough pleasantries. Kill them. Please don't put too many holes in the ladies' bodies that I'll have no use for."

Suddenly, Noreena came to life, charging Alexian, clawing at his face, spitting and snarling at him like some caged animal confronting its captor, her eyes wide and wild!

Alexian waved his arms frantically before him, swatting wildly at Noreena, doing his best to keep the savage Human female away from him. "Get her off me! Get her off me!"

The Volgarians dropped Rin's father, unceremoniously dumping his body to the floor, and moved for the wild Human female, struggling to pull her off Alexian.

Lizette joined the fray, charging the Volgarians, sinking her dagger deep into one of the Volgarian's exposed neck. Warm blood spurted out, showering the back of her hand and her wrist with dark liquid. She cut sideways, slicing a gaping hole in the Volgarian's flesh.

The Volgarian swatted at Lizette, knocking her into the nearby wall. Lizette grunted hard as she hit a painting and cracked the frame, but the picture remained hanging on the wall as she slid down the wall to land square on her butt on the floor. The Volgarian towered over her, his hand futilely trying to squelch the flow of blood spurting from his neck wound. Lizette grabbed a nearby pot that was sitting atop a marble pedestal and hurled the plant at the Volgarian. The ceramic container shattered on the Volgarian's chin, showering his face and eyes with blinding dirt.

Lizette was back on her feet quickly, sinking the blade into the Volgarian's throat. She shoved it deep, gritting her teeth tight as she thrust harder, her eyes narrow with fury, pushing the blade into the Volgarian all the way up to the hilt.

As Lizette and the first Volgarian fought, the second Volgarian finally got a grip on Noreena and yanked her roughly away from Alexian. The Volgarian squeezed her violently in his massive arms, leering down at her with his pustule-laden face as he tightened his deadly embrace. Noreena arched her back and lifted her head, crying out as her bones cracked under the immense squeezing pressure, and then she went limp, her body drooping lifelessly as the Volgarian loosened his grip on her. Blood oozed sickeningly out of her mouth, spilling down over her bottom lip, staining her chin with a deep crimson smear. Her eyes stared blankly.

As Lizette was battling the first Volgarian and Noreena was being murdered in the arms of the second Volgarian, Rin slammed his elbow into a mirror that was hanging in the hallway, breaking the glass into multiple shards. He grabbed a shard, quickly assessed its weight in his hand, then hurled it at the Volgarian holding Noreena's limp body. "Look here!" Rin shouted.

The Volgarian clutching Noreena looked up,

drawn by Rin's shout, to see the tip of the mirror shard an instant before it sank into his eye socket. He howled in pain, clutching at his eye; he lost his grip on Noreena and her body flopped down to the floor.

And then Lizette was there, attacking the second Volgarian, driving her blood-stained dagger into the second Volgarian's side between an opening in his armor. Rin scooped up more shards of the broken mirror and joined Lizette, slashing and cutting the Volgarian. The Volgarian waved his arms wildly, throwing Rin and Lizette off of him, shoving them away from him.

Rin was thrown into Alexian, the momentum knocking them both to the floor just as the Human was starting to flee. They wrestled on the floor, arms and legs flailing, fists swinging, feet kicking, each one struggling to get the upper hand. "Get him off me!" Alexian shouted, but there was no one to come to his aid.

Rin said nothing, concentrating on getting the upper hand in the fight. Rin managed to flip Alexian and get on top of him. They locked eyes for a moment as Rin managed to pin Alexian tightly to the floor with a firm forearm pressed hard against his throat. Rin held a mirror shard up before Alexian with his other hand. "Take a good look at yourself," Rin said. "It's the last chance you'll get." Rin slashed Alexian's throat, slicing through the exposed part of the Human's throat just below where his forearm was pressed into his neck. Blood splattered across the nearby wall. "The deal's off," Rin said. "You're out of business."

Lizette continued her attack on the second Volgarian, stabbing again and again, thrusting the blade into his side over and over, and finally he went down, dropping to his knees. Lizette stood near him, panting hard with the exertion of the battle. She bent over, feeling a winded pain flash through her side, and only took her gaze off the Volgarian for a second. But that was enough. The Volgarian quickly recovered and managed to grab a fallen shard of glass, driving it straight towards Lizette's face! There was no time for her to avoid the blow.

Then Rin was there, stopping the strike with a blocking forearm against the Volgarian's attacking forearm, stopping the blade mere millimeters from Lizette's throat!

The Volgarian turned to look at Rin, his remaining undamaged eye focusing on him, his other eye just a ragged pulpy mess of blood and loose tissue. Lizette took advantage of the distracting moment, sinking her blade into the Volgarian's throat. Warm blood pooled down over Lizette's hand. She shoved the blade in deeper. The Volgarian gurgled, and then the life just seemed to fade out of his good eye; he collapsed hard to the floor, landing atop numerous shards of shattered mirror glass with a loud crunching sound.

Everything was very quiet for a long moment. Lizette rose up and moved over to Alexian's body. She stared down at him for just a moment before spitting on his corpse. She turned to Rin, wiping the back of her mouth with her bloodied hand. She quickly grabbed at her tunic and wiped the blood from her mouth. She looked at Alexian again with blatant disgust, then turned back to face Rin. "You should've left him for me, Takan. He was mine."

Rin and Lizette stared at each other; both of them were splattered with blood, the crimson liquid staining their faces, their arms, their clothes.

"You don't look so good, Human," Rin said.

Lizette turned her gaze to Noreena, seeing her lying motionless in a heap on the floor. Her eyes widened in terror and Lizette moved quickly to her friend, kneeling down beside her. She grabbed at Noreena, scooping her hand behind her neck, raising Noreena's head up. "Talk to me, Noreena." But she knew Noreena was never going to talk to her again. Her eyes were open, glassy, vacant. Another oozing stream of blood dripped out of her slack lips. "I'm sorry, baby. I'm so sorry." She wiped the blood away from Noreena's mouth, cleaning her face as best she could. "I let you down again. I'm so sorry."

She looked up at Rin who was kneeling down only a few feet away, staring at the body of his father, the dead Takan's corpse lying in a heap on the floor. "We can't just leave them here," Lizette said. A tear dripped down Lizette's cheek.

Rin looked at the wet drop of moisture on her face curiously. He reached out and touched it. He studied the moist smear on his finger for a moment.

Lizette angrily wiped the wetness from her eyes and cheeks, her bloodied fingers just making more of a mess on her face. "They're tears, you dumb ass Takan."

Suddenly, the second Volgarian lurched to a

sitting position right next to them, howling in agony! His one good eye flitted about in its socket, as if the Volgarian was trying to get his bearings. His other socket oozed blood and pus.

Lizette jerked back, her eyes widening, grunting a startled gasp as she lurched away from the Volgarian.

Rin moved quickly, slamming a mirror shard into the Volgarian's face, sinking it deep into his undamaged eye socket. The Volgarian dropped hard back to the floor, almost falling straight back, and then lay still, the shard jutting out from his eye.

Again, everything was still for a long moment. Rin and Lizette kept a wary eye on the fallen Volgarians and the still body of Jason Alexian, but no one moved. They both struggled to slow their breathing, the heated flush of the battle starting to drain away out of their faces.

Finally, Rin quietly moved to his father's fallen body. He gently eased some of the brain matter that threatened to come out back into his father's skull. Then he gently lifted him up to cradle his corpse in his arms. He turned to Lizette. "Let's go," he said, his voice soft.

Lizette looked at him for a quiet moment. "Yeah, let's." She bent down to grab Noreena's body.

DIRT ROAD NEAR FALLING STREAM - NIGHT

Joktala and Alaysia, both armed to the teeth with daggers and throwing projectiles lodged into their clothing beneath belts or tucked into their boots, moved cautiously up to the edge of the Black Woods. They each carried a large leather bag, those too filled with weapons.

The Gatherers were already at the edge of the Black Woods waiting for them.

Joktala and Alaysia stopped and stared at the thick, thick blackness awaiting them as they reached the border of the Black Woods. The twin moons bathed the Takans and the Gatherers in their soft light, but the light from the two orbiting satellites did not appear to be able to penetrate more than a few feet into the Black Woods. The moonlight just seemed to stop as if there were a black curtain drawn around the entire expanse of Black Woods. The few visible trees that were closest to them were so dark they almost appeared to be made of shadows.

"We have to go in," Alaysia said. "If you don't get more leaf, you'll—"

Joktala impatiently nodded his head, making her cut off her words without him even making a sound. He winced, touching his bandaged throat.

But yet they still did not move any closer; they just stared at the coal-black trees. The Gatherers watched them, waiting quietly, patiently. T'rok cocked his head curiously at them, but made no sound.

"Do you think all those stories are true?" Alaysia asked. "Do you think the Black Woods are filled with monsters and demons and savage beasts?"

Joktala nodded softly, and then he stepped forward, moving into the Black Woods.

Alaysia watched him disappear into the blackness; it was as if the shadows just swallowed him up. One moment he was there in front of her, and the next moment he was just gone.

The Gatherers quickly followed Joktala, moving into the Black Woods, each one of them vanishing as quickly as Joktala had vanished. T'rok glanced back at Alaysia, waved his little furry hand at her to follow, then scampered after the others.

Alaysia stood alone in the night, glancing nervously around her, listening to the sounds of the forest, hearing the distant cries of animals. She turned back to face the eerie darkness of the Black Woods, then hurried forward to follow Joktala and the Gatherers.

BLACK WOODS - NIGHT

Joktala and Alaysia moved slowly through the black-trunked trees. The Gatherers led the way, but consciously stayed close to the two Takans, keeping quiet, their usually chattering and chittering completely absent. A strange pale white light illuminated the area, as if the dark trees themselves were giving off a bizarre glow despite how black they appeared, throwing eerie, dark shadows, distorted shadows, over everything.

Alaysia turned her head this way and that as they walked, trying to take in everything at once. "I couldn't see anything beyond the first few trees when we were outside the Black Woods, but now everything's all lit up," Alaysia said. "We don't even need a torch to see." She kept her voice low, soft, nearly whispering.

Joktala looked at her. He shifted the leather bag that was on his shoulder and drew out a piece of crumbled parchment from beneath his belt. He quickly scribbled on the parchment, then handed it to Alaysia. "It's like it's a different world in here," she said, reading his words aloud. She handed him the parchment back and he stuffed it under his belt.

They continued moving slowly forward, their gazes darting back and forth, feeling the need to be vigilant, their senses heightened by the very unfamiliar, unsettling surroundings. The ground was covered in various types of low foliage, interspersed with long stretches of bare dirt. The trees were somewhat widely spaced apart, sometimes growing in tight clusters, but mostly dozens of feet apart, giving them plenty of room to maneuver through the woods without having to get too near one of the black-trunked trees.

"Do you feel that?" Alaysia asked. "I can feel it through my boots. Like some weird tingling."

Joktala nodded.

Alaysia paused and stood motionless for a moment. "It feels like the ground is vibrating. Just a little, but I can feel it." Alaysia crouched down and put her hand on a bare patch of dirt, laying her palm flat against the ground. Her hand trembled, ever so slightly, but it still moved despite her best efforts to hold it completely still. "I'm trying to keep it still," she said to Joktala.

Joktala crouched down next to her. He also laid his palm flat against the ground and felt the same tingling sensation spread through his hand.

Alaysia looked over to him. "Do you really think it's some leftover…" her voice trailed off as she felt almost afraid to say the next word aloud. "Do you think it's… the old magic from the Alchemy Wars?" She hesitated again before continuing. "Like the stories say?"

Joktala looked at her but said nothing.

The Gatherers were stopped now, waiting patiently for them to continue, keeping quiet, just watching the two Takans. The pale light illuminating the area seemed to shift, the shadows falling over the Gatherers moving even though there was nothing else moving nearby that would cause the positions of the shadows to change.

Frightening noises, like animals snarling and fighting, came and went. The sounds were barely audible in the distance, but they all heard them.

Alaysia rose back up. She stepped hesitantly towards a nearby tree. She raised her arm, stretching her hand out towards the dark black bark of the tree.

Joktala rose back up, watching her curiously, wanting to see what would happen, not encouraging her to continue but also not trying to stop her.

Alaysia touched the black bark of the tree, first

putting the tips of her fingers against the trunk, then turning her wrist to flatten her palm against the bark. "Ohh!" she exclaimed and immediately pulled her hand back. It felt disturbing, odd, alien, as if something was alive inside the tree, like she was touching an animal but the animal did not want to be touched. She glanced down at her hand as if expecting to see something there, like a mark or a burn, something, but there was nothing on her palm, nothing on her fingers.

Joktala was quickly at her side, tugging on her arm, looking at her hand.

"It's okay," Alaysia said. "I'm okay." She looked at the tree, at its thickly grooved black bark. "It's... I don't know what it was. It felt... like... I don't know." She looked at Joktala. "Just don't touch them if you don't need to."

Joktala just looked at her.

"I don't like this place," Alaysia muttered. "Bad things happen in here. I just know they do."

Suddenly, the trees rustled wildly above them, the leaves snapping, the branches crackling, the sounds startling them. They all glanced up to see—

—gryfwings leaping from tree to tree. But these were not the same tiny, sleek-bodied animals they were used to seeing. They were larger, nearly twice the size of any gryfwings they had ever seen. Their wingspans were wider, their sinewy tails far longer. There was something about them that seemed deformed, distorted, as if they were grotesque aberrations of what a normal gryfwing was supposed to look like. The horde of gryfwings raced away from them, their pace fast and frantic.

"They sure are in a hurry," Alaysia said.

T'rok tugged at Alaysia's clothing, then pointed at the rapidly fleeing gryfwings, motioning for them to follow in the direction the animals were headed.

The other Gatherers began to run, fleeing in the direction the gryfwings were going.

A tremendous growl filled the woods, coming from the direction opposite where the gryfwings were headed. Joktala and Alaysia wasted no time in following the Gatherers' lead. They raced wildly through the woods, heading deeper into the heart of the Black Woods.

As he ran, Joktala glanced over his shoulder and saw the large silhouette of a strange beast lumbering through the woods, moving noisily amongst the trees. It had a vague similarity to a mulger, but this creature was nearly twice the size and its head appeared to hold a formidable set of teeth, with several tusks jutting out from its mouth. The beast must have found some prey because it stopped and made violently whipsawing motions with its head, as if it had just captured something and was ripping it to shreds with deadly claws and sharp teeth.

They continued running for a few moments longer, then slowed to rest as the creature faded from their view and the sounds of the beast were no longer audible.

"Okay, I think we just saw a savage beast," Alaysia said, her words coming out between the huffs and puffs of her labored breathing. "Now all we need are monsters and demons."

Joktala smiled grimly. He winced as he gingerly touched his bandaged throat. His ragged breathing sent sharp jabs of pain through him. He forced himself to calm down, to slow his breathing. The healing wound in his chest also flared up due to the exertion of running and he rubbed at it gingerly. He felt hot rivulets of sweat run down the side of his face.

"Are you okay?" Alaysia asked. She lifted the edge of her tunic and gently wiped away some of the sweat from Joktala's face.

Joktala nodded wearily.

Alaysia gently stroked his face and gave him a soft kiss on his lips. Joktala smiled weakly back at her.

Then, in the distance, Joktala saw a swirl of light, a pool of shifting colors. It seemed to float through the air, moving this way and that with no discernible pattern or destination. He grabbed Alaysia's arm and pointed at the swirling light.

The swirling circle of light was identical in shape and form to the structure Lizette had seen on the prison compound miniature diorama in Jason Alexian's study.

"By the Elders," Alaysia said, awe clearly audible in her tone. "It's a Worzon hole." She paused, and an even more incredulous tone crept into her voice. "They are real…"

Joktala nodded in agreement.

The pool of swirling light shifted direction, moving upwards.

Suddenly, a treebiter, one of the squirrel-like animals that fed on the bark of trees, lost its grip on a branch in a nearby tree, the little animal distracted by the swirling lights. The treebiter squealed in fright as it went tumbling towards the Worzon hole. This animal, too, seemed to be an aberration, its teeth much larger, much more pronounced, its tail flatter and longer.

"Look at the treebiter," Alaysia said excitedly, thrusting a pointing finger at the falling animal.

The treebiter twisted and turned in the air, doing whatever it could to avoid the spiraling pool of light, its tail swishing madly about as if it was trying to grab at the air, but there was no way for it to avoid the Worzon hole. The treebiter disappeared inside the swirling pool of colors, but did not come out the other side; it vanished into the Worzon hole.

Joktala and Alaysia exchanged a nervous glance, then turned away, moving away from the Worzon hole, heading deeper into the Black Woods. The Gatherers followed, still keeping quiet as they moved, all of their little faces filled with apprehension, and some filled with pure fear.

GROVE OF FIPPLE TREES – JUST INSIDE
TAKAN TERRITORY - NIGHT

Rin held a luckstone, a bright green gem with numerous facets, in his hand as he stared down into the hole where his father's corpse lay. He had his tunic back on. They knew they couldn't carry the dead bodies for miles, so they decided to bury them in a grove of fipple trees they had come across. The fipples, somewhat of a cross between an apple and a fig, weren't ripe yet, so they left them untouched despite how hungry they both were; eating unripe fipples only led to hours of misery and painful bowel movements.

Rin crouched down and put the gem in his father's hand and curled his dead fingers around the stone. Nearby, a torch stuck into the ground burned hotly, casting shadows onto the nearby fipple trees, the light bouncing off the dark brown waxy skins of the fruits and making them gleam. A long sharp rock was shoved into the ground near the torch, which Rin had used as a makeshift shovel to dig the grave. "For luck on the Journey," Rin said softly. He paused. "May it be a peaceful one." He rose to his feet to take one last look at his father.

Lizette stood quietly at Rin's side. She looked down at the gem in his father's fingers. "What's that?"

"It's a luckstone. For the Journey."

"The Journey?"

Rin nodded a soft nod. "Into the world beyond this one." He moved back down to his knees and began pushing the mounds of dirt that his digging had created back into the grave with his mud-streaked hands.

Lizette was silent for a moment, watching Rin finish burying his father. She then turned to look at Noreena lying naked in the hole she had dug. She looked at one of the daggers she had taken from the dead Volgarians and slid it out from behind her waistband to hold it in her hand. Then she bent down to put it in Noreena's hand. "For the

Journey." She curled Noreena's fingers around the handle of the blade. She leaned in closer and whispered, "Kick some ass." She kissed Noreena on the cheek and wiped a stray strand of hair away from her dead friend's face.

BLACK WOODS
STREAM NEAR COVERED BRIDGE - NIGHT

Joktala and Alaysia crouched behind a growth of brush, staring at—

—a dozen robed figures in the distance working the sweet leaf plants that were growing amidst the black trees, churning up the ground near the plants with rusted rakes. They have seen these figures before when the PowderKeeper fed the Gatherer memories into them.

Nearby, the decaying ruins of an ancient, heavily-weathered, covered-bridge spanned the nearby stream that separated Joktala, Alaysia, T'rok, and the other Gatherers from the robed figures. Several other crumbling, overgrown structures were visible behind them in the near distance. This growth of Black Woods had erupted around the remains of a war-ravaged village and the vegetation was slowly reclaiming all of the lands for itself, weaving its way through cracks in the buildings, sprouting thick black trunks straight through the roofs of old huts. The dark black trees emitted their eerie glow, bathing the entire area in a pale luminescence.

Joktala looked back to the other Gatherers, who were huddled together several feet behind Alaysia, looking afraid to move any closer. T'rok held on to Alaysia's leg, eyeing the robed figures with very nervous eyes.

Joktala moved to his weapon bag that he had set down on the ground earlier and pulled out several sharp-edged objects. These were five-sided throwing blades. He laid all eight of them down on the ground before him.

Joktala motioned to T'rok and the Gatherer reluctantly obeyed, moving away from Alaysia, releasing his grip on her leg. He moved closer to Joktala and lifted the flap on one of the small leather pouches at his waist. He removed a pinch of orange powder from his pouch. T'rok chattered impatiently at the other Gatherers and another Gatherer shuffled over to him and Joktala and took out a pinch of green powder from a pouch at his waist.

Both Gatherers sprinkled the powder over the throwing blades, making sure each of the eight blades received a dusting of the combined powders. Immediately, the blades glowed a deep orange, and lightning-shaped flashes of green light darted across their surfaces.

T'rok pointed to the crackling blades and chattered at Joktala, clearly urging him to pick them up.

Joktala picked up one of the glowing throwing stars, immediately feeling a surge of power emanating from the weapon as he held it pinched between two fingers. He quickly grabbed a few more of the throwing stars off the ground and moved over to Alaysia. He held the glowing blades out towards Alaysia, indicating with a jerking nod of his head for her to take them.

Alaysia stared at the sharp-pointed weapons in Joktala's hand, not yet taking them. "What do you want me to do with them?" she asked. Green flashes of light continued to dance across the surfaces of the blades and they each continued to give off a slight crackling sound.

Joktala pointed to the nearest robed figure and made a throwing gesture.

Alaysia looked at the robed figure, then frowned as she looked back to Joktala. "I couldn't hit him if he was sitting on top of me," Alaysia said.

Joktala scowled in frustration. He thrust the throwing stars again at Alaysia, motioning for her to hold on to them. She gingerly plucked them out of Joktala's hand and laid them flat in her open palm, careful not to prick herself on the sharp tips. They made her hand tingle, reminding her immediately of the vibrating sensation she had felt when she had put her hand against the forest floor.

Clutching a handful of the throwing blades, Joktala moved forward, cautiously stepping through the bushes, entering the deep shadows of the covered bridge. The blades pulsed and throbbed in Joktala's hand as he moved through the dark interior of the covered bridge. He shifted them behind his back as he moved, afraid their glow might give him away as he moved through the dim shadowy interior of the bridge. The others followed behind him. Joktala reached the edge of the bridge and cautiously peered out to see—

—a robed worker standing but a few yards away from him, working the soil with a rake. A few dozen yards away, another worker was harvesting a plant, stripping it of its leaves. He could still not make out their faces as they were all deeply shadowed within their wide hoods. What little he could see of their hands revealed pasty white fingers, fingers that may have never seen the darkening rays of the sun, especially if they spent most of their lives working in the dim light of the Black Woods.

A third robed worker finished filling a leather bag with sweet leaves and threw it onto a nearby cart that was already half-full with leaf-filled bags.

Joktala involuntarily licked his lips at the sight of the sweet leaves and absently touched at his bandaged throat. He eased off the bridge and moved nearer to the robed figure closest to him, quickly hiding behind a thick tree trunk, being careful not to brush up against the tree's bark, as the figure shifted attention to the next plant in the row. Then he inadvertently put his hand up against the black bark of the tree, but then immediately pulled his fingers away from the tree, understanding Alaysia's warning of doing their best to avoid touching them. It was as if he had touched the skin of an animal, almost like the rough texture of a frog's skin or the ribbed scales of a snake, and the animal had recoiled at his touch. He moved slightly back, moving away from the tree but still using its wide girth to hide behind. He returned his attention back to the figure working the plants.

The robed figure raised the rake and sifted through the dirt near the plant, tilling the area.

Joktala's eyes filled with determination as he clutched a blade firmly in his throwing hand. The weapon crackled softly as light danced across its surface. His fingers tingled with the promise of destructive power. He moved out from behind the tree and raised his hand to throw, when suddenly he froze, seeing—

—what was hiding beneath the dark robes. A Skeleton! The Skeleton stared at him with deep, empty sockets. Its skull-face was yellow-white in color, its teeth seeming to be locked into a permanently hideous grin in its mouthless, lipless jaw. It had no nose, only a dark slit where a nose had once been. Joktala could not tell if it had once been a Takan, a Human, a Volgarian, or perhaps even something else.

Alaysia gasped from her position at the edge of the covered bridge as she saw every robed Skeleton slowly turn in unison to face Joktala.

Joktala recovered from his initial shock and hurled the blade at the Skeleton near him. The five-pointed blade whistled shrilly as it whipped through the air, growing larger as it flew, its momentum unleashing its power, expanding as it sailed through the murky light, the flashes of green light growing brighter and brighter, pulsing faster and faster as it soared through the air, the blade reaching the size of a dinner plate just before it struck the Skeleton. Kablaam! The Skeleton detonated into thousands of shards of bone, its robe ripped to shreds by the violence of the explosion!

The Gatherers seemed to suddenly find their courage and they charged into the area, loping quickly forward on all fours. They quickly reached a row of plants and then maniacally began plucking as many sweet leaves as they could from their branches and thrusting them into their pouches.

Alaysia watched with terrified eyes as the other Skeletons converged quickly on Joktala. She eased off the covered bridge, cautiously moving closer.

Joktala fired off another throwing blade with a sharp toss of his wrist, but this one missed, the expanding weapon striking a tree near a Skeleton, blowing the trunk to smithereens. An odd wailing sound reverberated through the entire area, seeming to come from everywhere and nowhere all at the same time, as if the wind decided to push itself through every tree, through every branch, through every leaf, causing all of them to create sounds together in a weirdly harmonic moan.

Joktala's inadvertent strike on the tree had a positive effect on his skirmish with the robed figures as the thick tree toppled and crashed to the ground, leaving two crushed Skeletons in its wake, their bones crushed beneath the mighty trunk, their robes pinned flat to the ground.

A crunching sound behind Alaysia caused her to whirl and—

—stare into the bony face of a Skeleton! The Skeleton swung its rake at her and she dove away, narrowly missing being gored by the rake's rusty spikes. The throwing stars fell from her hand and clattered against each other as they hit the ground, but they did not have enough momentum behind them to fully activate them, so they did not expand nor explode.

Panicked, Alaysia clutched at a fallen throwing blade and hurled it at the Skeleton. Luckily, she missed the beast, otherwise she would have most likely been blown up along with it, and the expanding throwing star detonated against the wall of the bridge just behind them. The covered bridge teetered, then collapsed on its side as the rest of the bridge wall gave way under the strain.

Alaysia kicked at the approaching Skeleton, lashing out with her boot, delivering a solid blow to its knee area that caused the robed beast to buckle and nearly fall. This momentary respite gave her a chance to flee and she ran towards Joktala.

Joktala threw his last blade, blowing up the closest attacking Skeleton into a vaporizing cloud of bone and cloth, just as Alaysia reached his side. Suddenly, they heard a horrible, pain-filled screeching sound behind them and whirled to see—

—one of the Gatherers writhing on the bloodied tips of a Skeleton's rake. The Skeleton whipped the rake towards the ground, violently hurling the shrieking Gatherer into the dirt. The Gatherer hit the ground with a sickening thud and then immediately lay still.

Joktala looked around Alaysia, desperately searching for something, anything to strike with. He motioned wildly to her, then turned back towards their weapons bags to see—

—several Skeletons ripping through their weapon bags, emptying their contents to the ground, smashing them with their rakes.

Another Gatherer was bludgeoned to death trying to flee the area as a Skeleton smashed its tiny furry body repeatedly with the blunt end of a rake.

A Skeleton moved to strike T'rok with its rake but Joktala charged the undead monster, diving beneath its weapon, taking the blow meant for the little creature. The rake sunk deep into Joktala's shoulder and his face filled with intense pain. He opened his mouth to scream but no sound came out but a gurgling gasp and a sharp grunt.

"Joktala!" Alaysia screamed.

T'rok escaped, racing to join his brothers, helping them on, urging them to safety.

Joktala staggered to his feet just as another Skeleton drove its rake into his back. Again, he opened his mouth in a silent scream as he arched his back from the blow; only hoarse grunting, choking noises came out of his mouth. Pain fueled his anger and he whirled about to rip the rake from the second attacking Skeleton's bony fingers in a wave of savage fury. Joktala slammed the rake's spiked teeth into the Skeleton's head, shattering its skull. He continued fighting, a whirling tornado of hot rage, eventually pulverizing two more Skeletons into shards of lifeless bones with vicious strikes of the rake. The rake handle finally shattered as he delivered a tremendous blow to the skull of an attacking Skeleton. He stood for a moment with the ragged end of the rake in his hands, breathing heavily, his chest heaving. Blood seeped out of his new wounds, coating his back in a sea of red stains.

Alaysia hurried to Joktala's side as he staggered from the pain and loss of blood. Alaysia grabbed Joktala around the waist, helping him to stay on his feet. Blood immediately oozed onto her clutching arm, streaming down from his wounds.

T'rok looked at the two Takans over his shoulder as he led the other Gatherers away, and stopped when he saw how wounded Joktala was. He chittered at the other Gatherers, getting them to stop. He pointed back at the Takans, then motioned for the other Gatherers to follow him back towards Alaysia and Joktala. T'rok didn't wait for their reaction; he just immediately turned about and started running back towards the Takans. The other Gatherers followed T'rok's lead, scampering after him.

T'rok chattered loudly at Alaysia as he reached her side and she glanced down to see him holding a tiny furry hand full of sweet leaf. They were different from the bits of sweet leaf Joktala normally consumed; the red veins running through the leaves in T'rok's hand were much thicker and fatter. Alaysia took the leaves and fed them to Joktala, forcing him to eat them by shoving them deep into his mouth and squeezing at his jaw to make him move his teeth.

Immediately after a few seconds of chewing the potent leaves, and especially after his first swallow of the fluids his chewing of the leaves created, Joktala's body tensed and his gaze started to swim. He struggled to shake off the effects of this powerful variant of the sweet leaf, but he had a hard time staying focused. He felt vibrantly alive and overwhelmingly exhausted all at the same time. He could feel the pulsing throbs in his back, each rake tip wound like a separate knife cut, each one aching with intense flaring pain.

The remaining Skeletons drew closer, the robed figures now circling them; some of them clutched rakes, some spades, and some were empty-handed with their skeletal fingers curling into bony claws. But then suddenly the Skeletons stopped. They abruptly ceased their motions as if some puppet master pulling their strings called for a temporary halt in the action.

Alaysia looked on with nervous eyes at this odd lack of movement. Joktala, now leaning heavily on Alaysia, was having a hard time staying focused on anything. For him, everything was still moving, everything around him still swimming with weirdly melting motions.

A Volgarian stepped out of nearby deep shadows. He was dressed in what appeared to be a uniform of sort, with a dark green tunic, dark green breeches, and black leather boots. His purple-black face was laced with scars and half of his right ear was missing. The Volgarian stared at Joktala and the others for a long moment. "Gut them. Gut them all and bring me their corpses," the Volgarian commanded.

Joktala, Alaysia, and the Gatherers drew tighter together as the Skeletons again started moving closer. Joktala was bleeding profusely from his savage wounds, barely able to stand, but some energy and healing strength from the sweet leaves finally began to revitalize him. He was able to stand on his own without Alaysia holding him up, and his vision had started to clear.

Then, one of the Gatherers started squealing excitedly, pointing into the distance. Joktala followed his pointing finger to see—

—the Worzon hole shimmering in the distance just beyond three Skeletons. It was low to the ground, nearly touching the leaves and dirt of the forest floor.

Appearing almost drunk, his movements wildly exaggerated, Joktala grabbed Alaysia's arm, whirling her around to see the Worzon hole. He pointed at the Worzon hole, his finger insistent in its sharp stabbing motion.

"No way, Joktala!" she protested. "We don't know where that Worzon hole leads or what's inside or what even happens if we go into it."

Joktala pointed to the approaching Skeletons, waving his hand violently at them, then pointed to the Worzon hole even more emphatically.

"Elders curse you!" Alaysia snapped at him.

The Gatherers chattered amongst themselves, exchanging powders from their pouches, pooling the small grains into a tiny pile on T'rok's open palm. T'rok squeezed his hand tight, compressing the powders.

Joktala felt something tugging at his pant leg and he glanced down to see T'rok holding a pellet of some sort. His vision swam for a moment, but he forced himself to focus. Joktala was really wired up, his actions wild and frenetic. He took the offered pellet, staring at it for a moment, not knowing what to do with it, trying to keep it in focus. Then he popped it into his mouth.

The Gatherers shrieked in protest, frantically

waving at him to stop. But it was too late. Joktala had already swallowed it. The Gatherers tried to bury themselves in the ground, scratching at the dirt, then quickly covered their heads with their arms when they realized they were barely making any headway and wouldn't be able to dig a hole deep enough to save them from what was coming.

Joktala stared down at the cowering Gatherers with confused eyes.

"I don't think you were supposed to eat that," Alaysia said.

The Skeletons drew closer, some of them now holding their rakes like swords or clubs.

The Volgarian commander watched from the distance.

Joktala looked at his hands, turning them palms up, then flipping them over. He glanced over at Alaysia, shrugging.

T'rok chanced a peek at Joktala through his arms, taking his arms away from their protective position over his head. When the little Gatherer saw that nothing was happening to the Takan, he lowered his arms even further and lifted his head up, cocking it to stare quizzically at Joktala.

Wham! Tendrils of lightning shot out from Joktala's fingers, the hot electric bolts blasting into the dirt nearby! Joktala's face twisted into a horrible grimace of pain as the surge of energy exploded through him. For a brief moment, he could not control his hands and the lightning blasts shot every which way.

T'rok dove for cover amidst his fellows, again throwing his arms over his head. Alaysia dove to the ground to join the Gatherers huddled together in fear.

A Skeleton was right on them now and Joktala turned towards it, raising his fingers towards the approaching black robed figure. The electricity leaping from Joktala's fingers speared the Skeleton, blasting its joints to bits. Joktala whirled, fighting the agony burning inside him, and struck out at another attacking Skeleton, this time able to directly aim the strike. Shards of bone clattered loudly against each other as the Skeleton detonated. Then he spun towards the Worzon hole, blasting the three Skeletons near the swirling circle of glowing light in rapid succession, pulverizing them with spearing bolts of energy; a robe covering one of the Skeletons burst into flames. He spun again to his left, aimed with his fingers, and blew another Skeleton into shards of splintered bones and misty shreds of fabric.

Then, just as abruptly as the power had appeared from within Joktala, it vanished, leaving Joktala with charred, smoking fingertips. He stood motionless for a long moment, staring at the tips of his smoldering fingers. And then he fell hard to the ground, just collapsing in a heap.

Alaysia quickly moved to his side, trying to get him to stand up. "Come on, Joktala! Get up! Get up!"

But Joktala was going nowhere. He struggled to get a breath and a hint of smoke came out of his mouth. Then, the Gatherers were at his side, tugging at his shirt, his pants, pulling him away from the still approaching Skeletons, pulling him towards—

—the Worzon hole.

Alaysia hesitated a moment, but then joined the Gatherers in their efforts, tugging and yanking and pulling on Joktala's unconscious body. They reached the Worzon hole.

And went through.

FOREST TRAIL NEAR FALLING STREAM - DAY

The sun was visible on the horizon and only one moon remained in the sky at this time of day. Rin and Lizette walked quietly side by side, both absorbed in their own thoughts.

"Listen, Takan—"

"Rin. You can call me Rin."

"Yeah. Okay, Rin. I'm Lizette. Listen, I usually don't get involved in this shit, but you helped me out and I don't like owing anybody anything."

Rin stopped walking and looked at her, waiting for her to continue.

Lizette paused and turned to face him. "You know that place the Volgarian talked about. Ashenwall, or something like that? Well, I saw some kind of map in the house. They're really building it."

"You saw a map of it?"

Lizette nodded. "Yeah. A layout, some kind of building plan."

"Where? Where did you see this map?" There was a sense of urgency to Rin's questions.

"In some room in the house. Like a study or something. It had a bunch of books in it."

Rin quickly turned back in the direction of the house.

Lizette grabbed his arm, stopping him. "Hey, forget it."

Rin shrugged off her hand. "I need to see that map. The Clan Council needs to see it."

"Forget it. I burned it with my fire blade."

Rin frowned. "You burned it?"

"Hey, I was burning everything," Lizette said defensively. "I didn't even know what the hell it was at the time."

"What was it? What did this map look like?"

"It wasn't really a map. It was more like a miniature layout. It looked like some kind of damned fortress to me. A bunch of buildings. Guard towers everywhere. Fences."

"You said it was a map," Rin said.

Lizette's temper flared. "I didn't mean map. It was some kind of construction plans or something. It showed the buildings, but tiny. Like toy houses for children."

Rin clenched his jaw, but said nothing.

"Hey, I'm sorry," Lizette said, calming herself. "I didn't know what it was. And it might not even be the same thing as this Ashenwall they were talking about."

Rin remained silent. "But you think it is," he said after a moment.

Lizette nodded. "My gut tells me it is, yes. They're building something big."

"Where are they building it?" Rin asked.

Lizette shook her head. "I don't know." She stared off into the distance, then looked back to Rin. "Look, I doubt Alexian and his Volgarian attack pack were the only ones involved in this. This thing they are building is too big. I don't think he was smart enough to run something that big." She paused. "They're gonna come after you if they find out a Takan's in on their dirty little secret."

"They could come after you, too," Rin said.

Lizette shrugged. "I don't think so. Seems more like a Takan Volgarian problem to me."

Rin said nothing. After a moment he said, "I guess this is where we part ways."

She drew one of the Volgarian daggers she had taken from them after their fight in Alexian's house, pulling it out from her waistband. She held the handle out to Rin. "You need one of these?"

Rin shook his head.

Lizette was quiet for a moment. "Take care of yourself then."

"You, too."

Lizette flipped the dagger in her hand and slid it smoothly back into place at her waist. "Oh, you know I will."

Rin watched Lizette walk away.

WORZON HOLE - TEMPLE OF HUNAK - DAY

Joktala's eyes slowly opened. He blinked a few times, realizing that he was lying on his back. There was a domed ceiling far above him, the ceiling appearing to be made of white marble or some other very smooth-looking stone. He eased himself up to a sitting position, noting that a pile of soft blankets was laid out beneath him. The room was circular in shape, the smooth stone walls sloping up to the high domed ceiling far above. He glanced around the large room, seeing—

—that he was inside a large temple of sorts, the room wide and spacious. Before him, stone sculptures of myriad types of beings lined one of the walls. He saw statues of Humans, Takans, a Volgarian, Scitites, a PowderKeeper, and dozens of other races. They were all positioned on marble pedestals, each one life-size in scale, each one exquisitely detailed. Some of the races had statues of both males and females, while others had only a male or a female or some indeterminate gender.

T'rok jumped onto his lap, startling him.

"Hey! You—" Suddenly, Joktala froze, realizing that he could talk again. He quickly put his hand to his throat to find that it was healed, the bandages gone. "I can talk." He grabbed the little Gatherer and gave him a big hug. "I can talk again!" His words came out a little roughly at first, but quickly smoothed out the more he spoke. "I can talk!" That's when he finally realized he was wearing no clothing. "And I'm naked!"

T'rok chattered back at him and squirmed in his grasp. Joktala set him gently down.

Then, Joktala noticed that his charred fingers had healed as well. He immediately poked at his chest, where his wound had once been, but there were no bandages covering the area, and there was no pain, not even a twinge. He flexed his shoulder blades, squeezing them together, and quickly grinned as he realized the wounds in his back were gone as well. All of his wounds had vanished. He rubbed his hands excitedly over his healed flesh and looked at T'rok with a bright gleam in his yellow eyes. "I don't know what this place is, but I like it!"

THE VILLAGE OF FALLING STREAM
A TAKAN VILLAGE - DAY

Rin walked briskly through the Takan village of Falling Stream. All around him, Takans were working, gossiping, living out their day, blissfully unaware of the horrors lurking behind the scenes of their tranquil lives. Several Takan children raced past him, hitting a ball with a stick. Rin watched them wistfully, pausing in his quick pace for just a brief moment, then hurried on his way.

TAKAN SCHOOL - DAY

Rin walked down the empty hallway, passing classroom doors, hearing the sounds of students at work coming from some of the open doorways. He stopped before a wall filled with sketches of young Takans, drawings of all the students who had attended classes at the school. He found a drawing of Alaysia, Joktala, and himself, all positioned beneath the picture of their Teacher, an older Takan male named Nakarian.

Rin heard another Teacher's voice, a female Takan voice, drift out of the nearby classroom. "The Rangers have discovered a new growth of Black Woods near Luxen Pass," the female voice said. "Please avoid that area until we tell you otherwise.

Rin moved on. He walked up to an open classroom door and peered cautiously inside, craning his neck to look into the room but keeping his body back as far from the doorway as he could to avoid being seen.

*****

Teacher Nakarian, whose sketch Rin had just seen in the hallway, sat before his students, a group of young male and female Takan children, ranging from seven to thirteen seasons old. Nakarian had aged well; only a few more new wrinkles were visible on his face that weren't visible in the portrait in the hallway.

"My mother says the Black Woods are full of strange plants and that's where the PowderKeepers get all their magic from," one young male student said.

Nakarian scowled at the student. He rose up from his seat and stood before the class. "I'll have no talk of PowderKeepers in this classroom, do you understand me? Only the desperate or the deranged use their..." He paused as he searched for a word. "...services." He glanced over his classroom, looking from student to student. "And, please, let's stop this foolish talk of magic once and for all.

There is not, nor has there ever been, such a thing."

"Then how do you explain the Black Woods?" a young female student asked.

"The Black Woods are the lingering aftermath of the great Alchemy Wars," Nakarian said. "It wasn't magic. It was the misuse of knowledge. The misuse of science. They are a reminder to us of the evil and violence of warfare. They only grow where horrible atrocities occurred. They only spread where the dark weapons of the Worzons were used. They only thrive where the blood-soaked memories of murder stain the soil." Nakarian paused, again looking from student to student, making sure each young Takan was paying attention to him. "That is why we do not enter them."

"A friend of my Clan brother said his father's blood sister saw a Worzon hole at the edge of the Black Woods near Mirahk village," another male student chimed in.

Several students fidgeted uncomfortably in their chairs.

"Do you think there are any Worzons still alive?" another female student asked.

Nakarian looked at her with a serious expression on his face. "For all of our sakes, let's hope not. Their Alchemy Wars almost destroyed the world hundreds of seasons ago. We're all better off without them."

"What were they like? The Worzons," a young male asked.

Nakarian made a foul face. "They were all monstrous beasts with a taste, a need, an unquenchable desire for blood." He paused between each declaration, as if searching for the words he thought would have the most effect on his students. "They kept thousands of beings as slaves, feeding on hundreds a day to satisfy their ugly appetites. They destroyed the Braktu and the Verloi races entirely in their wars, annihilating their kind completely."

"My father's father's father said the Worzons created the world and all the creatures in it," a female student said.

Nakarian scoffed. "That's ridiculous and absurd. The only thing the Worzons created is the horror of the Black Woods."

A younger female student raised her hand. "Teacher?"

Nakarian looked over to the questioning student.

"I think someone is spying on us," she said. She pointed to the doorway to the classroom.

Nakarian glanced where she was pointing, and then headed for the door.

*****

Nakarian stepped out into the hallway.

"Greetings, Teacher Nakarian," Rin said. "It appears you have not lost your flair for the dramatic." He grinned at his former teacher. Teacher Nakarian had always been overly melodramatic in his presentations when he had taught him, Joktala, and Alaysia, so it was oddly comforting to see that he had barely changed at all. It was one thing that still seemed normal after all the craziness that had just happened to him.

Nakarian looked at Rin, studying him. Suddenly, recognition flashed across his eyes and his expression darkened dramatically. "Leave me be, Rin Grinto. No more of your pranks!"

Rin took a step back, holding his empty hands up. "No tricks. I need to talk to you, Teacher. It's important."

Nakarian glanced behind Rin, searching. "Where's that bastard friend of yours?"

Rin lowered his hands slowly. "That's one of the reasons I'm here. He's gone. Joktala... He's... dead."

Nakarian looked towards the heavens, letting out a satisfied sigh. "The Elders have blessed me."

Rin forced himself not to react to Nakarian's remark, keeping the scowl off his face as best he could. He took a hesitant step forward. "Teacher, I—"

Nakarian shook his hand at him, cutting him off. "I've had peace and quiet for eight years without you and your friends playing nasty tricks on me. I intend to keep it that way."

Rin stepped forward quickly, grabbing Nakarian's wrist, forcing him to pay heed to his words. "Listen to me! Alaysia's gone, too! I think the Volgarians took her." He paused. "Or killed her." Rin let go of his grip on Nakarian's hand. "I need your help."

Nakarian's angry eyes softened at the mention of Alaysia. "Alaysia's gone?"

Rin nodded. "I went to her house but she wasn't there. They broke in." Rin paused, glancing down at the floor. "There was blood everywhere." Rin looked back up at Nakarian, his eyes beseeching his old teacher to help. "I came to you because I didn't know where else to turn."

Nakarian frowned. "Then you must be desperate."

Please," Rin said. "We're all in danger."

Nakarian studied Rin for a moment, saw the earnest truth in his eyes. "Who's in danger?"

"All of us," Rin said. "You. Me. Every Takan."

Nakarian eyed Rin skeptically.

WORZON HOLE - TEMPLE OF HUNAK - DAY

"**A**laysia?" Joktala's voice echoed in the large chamber, making him suddenly apprehensive about making so much noise. He moved slowly about the chamber, treading the smooth stone floor lightly, studying the various statues that filled the room as he looked for his companion. He called out Alaysia's name again, this time keeping his voice low. He had found his clothes and boots in a pile near the blankets and had put them back on. His tunic and breeches were still stained with dirt and some darkened patches of dried blood, but they at least seemed to have been cleaned. "Alaysia," he called out again.

There was no answer.

He paused before the stone statue of the male Takan, studying it. He tried to think if it reminded him of anyone he knew, but it didn't really. Maybe the sculpture looked a bit like a young version of Teacher Nakarian, but that was about as close as the face on the statue got to someone he knew.

T'rok pointed to a shadowed doorway leading deeper into the structure, then headed for it. The Gatherer paused after a few steps and turned back to Joktala, chittering at him, waiting for him to follow.

Joktala was too absorbed in his exploration of the room to pay much attention to T'rok. He continued to study his surroundings, frowning at the Volgarian statue. He felt an immense urge to urinate on it, but kept himself in check. He wondered if any of the robed Skeletons had followed them into the Worzon hole, but it did not appear that they had because there was no sight of them anywhere he looked.

"Alaysia?" His voice became louder again, more insistent on a response.

The room was silent but for the softly echoing repetition of Alaysia's name bouncing back down from the high domed ceiling.

T'rok chattered loudly, motioning for Joktala to come with an insistent wave of his furry hand.

Then, a piercing scream filled the air, coming from the direction of the doorway where T'rok stood.

Joktala whipped his head toward the source of the cry. "Alaysia!"

Joktala and the Gatherer raced into the darkened doorway. They burst into the adjoining room to see—

—Alaysia lying naked on the ground, a strange creature towering over her. The creature looked similar to a PowderKeeper, with six tendril-like arms, small eyes and a large head, but with definitely a more Human-like appearance. And this creature was about twice as big as any PowderKeeper they had ever seen. Alaysia's screaming had stopped and Joktala could see that numerous tendrils of the creature were attached to her forehead.

The creature looked up at Joktala and made an unintelligible clacking sound which slowly transformed into understandable words. "Takan. How did you come here?" The creature's voice had a slightly lower pitch than the Takans, a male deepness to it that seemed to reverberate with oldness, the tone hinting that this creature was well beyond their age.

"Let her go," Joktala demanded. He took a step forward, but the Gatherers crowded around him, keeping him back, pushing at his legs to prevent him from getting too close to the large creature.

"As you wish. I am finished." The creature released his tendrils from Alaysia's forehead and they wiggled and danced in the air as he retracted them.

Alaysia gasped and put her hands to her head.

Joktala gritted his teeth and glared at the large being. "What did you do to her?"

"I finished what I had intended to do so long ago," the creature said, his voice almost wistful as if he were absently just musing to himself.

Joktala's jaw tightened and his eyes grew hotter. "Look, you jreck, I'm gonna—"

"It's okay." Alaysia held her hand up to Joktala

as she sat up, her motion silencing him for the moment. "It's okay. I'm all right. I feel a little tired, a little dizzy, but I'm all right." Then she paused to stare at Joktala. "Hey, you can talk."

Joktala touched his throat. "I woke up and it was healed."

"And your hands, too," Alaysia said, looking over at his fingers. "They're not burned anymore." She looked up at him and smiled.

Joktala looked down at his fingers, wriggling them. "Yeah." He moved to Alaysia's side, crouching down next to her.

"I healed you," the creature said. "You Takans have remarkable endurance."

Joktala and Alaysia turned to look up at the creature. Joktala's rage faded, his expression softening.

"And all that sweet leaf you ingested didn't hurt your chances of survival, either," the creature said. He paused and his tendrils stopped moving, as if freezing in place as he lost himself in his thoughts. "Wonderful stuff, that sweet leaf. I wish I had thought of that one." He looked back to Joktala and his tentacles started waving again. "A lesser being would have been dead from the wounds I found all over your body."

T'rok moved up to Joktala and Alaysia. Alaysia gave the little Gatherer a warm smile and gently caressed the fur around his face. The other Gatherers huddled nearby, keeping together as a group a few feet away. Alaysia looked back up at the creature. "Where are we?" she asked. She was still sitting on the floor, still working up the energy to get back to her feet. Joktala remained crouched down at her side, holding her hand.

"You are in my home."

"You live in the Worzon hole?" Joktala asked, incredulous.

The creature blinked slowly at Joktala. "I am Hunak. I am Worzon."

Joktala and Alaysia exchanged nervous glances. Joktala looked down at Alaysia's nudity, then back up to her face. "I think you better get dressed."

HOME OF TEACHER NAKARIAN - DAY

Rin and Nakarian were sitting in Nakarian's living room inside his modest Takan home. The chairs were covered in leather, overstuffed with wool, comfortable enough to easily fall asleep in before a warm hearth on a relaxing day, but Rin was in an agitated state far away from relaxation; he wondered if he would ever be able to relax again.

A fire burned inside a fireplace nearby. Rows of wooden shelves lined the wall opposite the fireplace, the shelves filled with leather-bound books. Nakarian was smoking a long-stemmed pipe that stretched from his lips to the floor. He exhaled a thick cloud of yellow-white smoke. His legs were stretched out long before him, clearly in a much more relaxed state than Rin.

Rin leaned forward in his chair and waved the smoke away from his face. "I came to you because I need to get a message to the Council and I know you are friends with a few of its members."

"But you said this Human, this Jason Alexian, said the Council already knows about what the Volgarians are doing," Nakarian said.

Rin frowned at Nakarian. "Yes, I said that. But do you really believe the Takan Council would condone such a thing?"

Nakarian was quiet for a moment, smoking his pipe. "The Council will need to talk to the Human female," he finally said.

"Why?"

"She saw the layout of this..." He looked to Rin.

"Ashenwall."

Nakarian nodded. "Yes. She saw the layout. A map or something, you said. She needs to tell us more. She needs to tell us all she knows."

Rin shook his head. "She doesn't know any more. I already asked her."

Nakarian's relaxed face took on a more tightened look as a stern expression steeled his features. "We won't be asking her."

Rin frowned, confused.

"Bring her to a PowderKeeper. He can get us the information we need," Nakarian said. The teacher tapped at the edge of his forehead.

Rin stared at his former teacher, trying to keep the shock out of his expression. "I thought only the deranged or the desperate used their services."

Nakarian looked straight at Rin. "It appears to me that you might easily qualify in both categories."

Rin's frown deepened. He looked away from Nakarian. "I wouldn't even know where to find her."

Nakarian put his lips to his pipe, but didn't inhale because a thought interrupted him. "Humans have a strong need to visit their dead, especially when their corpse is still fresh. Do you remember where she buried her friend?"

Rin stared at his teacher. "Yes, right next to my father."

WORZON HOLE - TEMPLE OF HUNAK - DAY

Joktala grabbed Alaysia's hand and tugged her closer to him. She was now dressed again, her clothing still stained and tattered but a little cleaner now than when they had first entered the Worzon hole. They slowly backed away from the Worzon, their booted feet making soft clacking sounds against the stone floor as they moved.

The Gatherers remained where they were nearby, watching, keeping quiet.

"What are you doing?" Alaysia asked.

"It's a Worzon!" Joktala exclaimed. "They drink blood and eat raw flesh. Didn't you ever pay attention in Teacher's class?"

"Yes, but I'm surprised you did," Alaysia said.

Joktala frowned at her. "Just move." He kept a firm grip on Alaysia's hand as he slowly backed away, pulling her away from the Worzon along with him. T'rok kept close by, moving along with them.

Hunak moved with them as well, keeping pace. Joktala noticed the Worzon had feet somewhat like the PowderKeeper's feet, flat pads that seemed to have dozens of tiny toes beneath them propelling him in the direction he needed to go. Hunak watched them with his tiny beady eyes as he followed them. His tendrils darted close to them, then pulled back, making Joktala involuntarily start with a sharp jerk away from any tendril that got too close to him.

The other Gatherers slowly followed. None of them seemed to be scared or alarmed by the large Worzon, just curious.

"He kind of looks like a PowderKeeper, doesn't he?" Alaysia whispered to Joktala.

"Yeah, a big fat one," Joktala said flippantly. He whipped his head left, then right, looking for a way out as they backed away from the Worzon.

They moved back into the large outer chamber where all of the stone statues of the various races were located. "I don't see a way out," Joktala said. He quickly scanned the floor around them. "Do we have any weapons?" He continued to scan the area as they moved past the Human female statue, then the Human male statue. "Maybe the Gatherers still have some powders we can mix to help us get out of here."

The Worzon and the other Gatherers followed them into the large room. The other Gatherers spotted small statues of their race situated on pedestals nearby and they all started chattering excitedly at each other, pointing at the finely detailed sculptures of their kind.

Suddenly, T'rok darted away from Joktala and Alaysia, moving towards the Worzon.

"Hey, stay here! T'rok!" Joktala shouted at him, but the Gatherer kept on going.

T'rok scampered towards Hunak. He climbed up the statue of the Human female that the Worzon was near, and then jumped onto Hunak's shoulder. The little Gatherer chattered excitedly at the Worzon.

The Worzon touched a tentacle to T'rok, probing him gently on his furry shoulder, then chattered back in what sounded like the same language. They exchanged a few sentences, with T'rok pointing to the Takans as they talked. Then the Worzon wrapped its tentacle around T'rok, gripping the Gatherer tightly.

Joktala clenched his fist and took a step forward towards the Worzon. "Hey!"

Hunak looked over at Joktala and Alaysia. "Fear is not necessary."

"Are you going to eat us?" Alaysia asked. She and Joktala stopped moving and just stared at the Worzon.

"No." Hunak gently lowered T'rok back to the ground and unfurled his tentacle so the Gatherer could move back towards Joktala and Alaysia.

The Worzon stared intently at the two Takans. "You must forgive my fascination. I did not expect to see you flourish as you are. You were my last and I never had the chance to teach you your full potential." His tentacles danced and weaved in the air.

Joktala and Alaysia were quiet for a moment.

They looked at each other, not sure of what was going on. Joktala turned confused eyes to Hunak. "We were your last what?"

"My last creation," Hunak said.

The Worzon saw Alaysia glancing at all of the statues surrounding her, saw her scowl at the Volgarian statue, then move on to look at the Humans, Gatherers, Takans, and many others. Her gaze stopped on another Human-like race with scaly, reptilian skin. "That is a Verloi," Hunak said. "They are all gone now. Destroyed in the Great War."

"The Great War?" Alaysia asked.

"I think he's talking about the Alchemy Wars," Joktala said. "The Worzon civil war."

"Yes," Hunak said. "The Alchemy Wars. An apt name for it. Hundreds of seasons ago, we, the Worzons, were separated into dozens of factions. We all wanted to control the destiny of the world. We all thought we knew what was best for the future." He paused. "We were all wrong. All we ended up doing was destroying everything we had ever created. We exterminated race after race in our struggles for domination."

Hunak pointed to the statues with his tentacles. "I created these as a memorial for all the races that ever inhabited the world." He lowered one of his tentacles. "Now only a few still survive." The rest of Hunak's raised tentacles dropped to his side. "The deadly powders we used in the Great War stripped all of us of the ability to create new life. Our abilities became as barren and sterile as our souls. We can no longer create more life. We can only watch it die and wait for our own eventual deaths."

Joktala and Alaysia were quiet, still trying to absorb and assess what the Worzon was trying to tell them.

The Worzon stared quietly back at them.

"What's that?" Alaysia asked.

The Worzon followed Alaysia's pointing finger to see—

—a hideous winged beast with a feral, snarling troll sitting in a saddle atop its back.

"A Seeker Destroyer," Hunak answered. "A terrible creature. A relentless hunter. It wouldn't stop until either it or its prey were dead. Be thankful they, too, are gone from the world. They were our ultimate destructive creation, given life only to spread death."

"Hold on here," Joktala said. "You keep saying our creations."

The Worzon motioned with his tentacles to all of the statues surrounding them. "Yes. Our creations."

Joktala's face filled with disbelief. "The Volgarians, the PowderKeepers, the Gatherers? You created them? You created us? The Takans?"

"The Worzons created them, yes. Not just me. There are others like me." His tentacles froze in mid-air. "At least I believe there are still others. I can only assume some others have survived because I have heard of other Worzon holes still existing." His tentacles waved in the air again, again pointing to various stone statues. "We created them to share the world with us." Hunak paused. "They, you, were our playthings, our amusements, our companions, until our bitter rivalries turned them into weapons and soldiers of destruction."

Joktala stared with numb shock at the Worzon, trying to comprehend what the creature was saying. Then, suddenly, Joktala burst out laughing.

Alaysia frowned at him. "What? What's so funny?"

"It just figures. Rin was the one always looking for something, searching for something bigger and greater than himself, and I'm the one who finds it." His laughter faded and his face took on a somber earnestness. "Elders curse us, Alaysia. We found the Great One."

Alaysia and Joktala stared at the Worzon for a long moment.

"Kind of disappointing, isn't he?" Alaysia muttered to Joktala.

The Worzon waved his tentacles wildly about them. "You must tell me why you have come into my home. The world outside is poisonous to me now so I cannot leave my home ever again. A simple breath of air outside my home would choke me to death. Lately I have only received visits from unfortunate animals. And they are not much use for learning what is really happening in the world."

"It was the only way we could escape the Skeletons," Alaysia said.

It was Hunak's turn to look confused as his beady eyes shriveled down to an even smaller size. "Skeletons?"

Alaysia nodded. "They were attacking us in some Black Woods and we had nowhere to go except into the Worzon hole. Into here. Into your home."

Joktala looked at Hunak. "What are the Black Woods really? We've been told to stay away from them, to fear them, ever since we were younglings."

Hunak did not answer right away. His tentacles paused, then started to move again. "The Great War had a devastating effect on the world," he said. "We unleashed great powers in our civil war, powers we didn't understand. The Black Woods were created by that war. The residue of our dark powers seeped into the soil of the world." Hunak paused. "And the Black Woods were born. From what little I understand of what is now happening outside my home, you can find pockets of them all over the world."

Joktala looked at Alaysia. "Maybe Teacher did tell us the truth for once."

Alaysia looked at Hunak. "We touched some of the trees in the Black Woods. They seemed like they were alive. Are all the trees in the Black Woods alive?"

Hunak's tentacles rose up, then drooped. "Every pocket of Black Woods will hold its own mysteries. Seasons ago, when a Human entered into my home, he told me of a woods that were filled with black trees made of stone, and here you tell me of black trees that are alive." Hunak paused. "I don't think any pocket of Black Woods will be the same. There are thousands of combinations of the powders, tens of thousands, and during the Great War we were trying them all to get an upper hand against each other. We have stained the earth with their residue."

Joktala was quiet for a moment. "So the residue from the powders is like some magic fertilizer? Making the Black Woods grow where the powders were used?"

Hunak waved his tentacles up and down. "Yes. Every battle involved different powders, different combinations of powders. So that is why every Black Woods will be different."

They were all quiet for a moment.

"You must tell me what else is happening," Hunak said.

"The Volgarians steal our dead from their graves," Alaysia said.

This clearly upset the Worzon. "Volgarians. I never did like them. Crass and vulgar things. Purely created for gross amusements. They weren't one of mine." Hunak waved his tentacles in the air as he studied the two Takans standing before him. A strange, calculating look came into his eyes. "Come. You must eat to find your strength."

GROVE OF FIPPLE TREES – JUST INSIDE
TAKAN TERRITORY - DAY

Lizette stood before Noreena's grave, holding food in her hand, a small loaf of bread, some dried meat. She set the food down on the grave, putting it directly atop the slightly rounded mound of dirt that served as Noreena's final resting place. Then she placed a shining jewel into the dirt atop the grave, pushing the gem beneath the surface, placing it right about where Noreena's heart would be if she pushed the gem down far enough into the grave. "For luck. May your Journey be a peaceful one." Her voice was soft, gentle.

Immediately, a roachrat scurried out from beneath a large rock. The small vermin moved right up to the food, sniffing at the dried meat. In an instant, the roachrat's head was severed from its body.

"I ain't in a sharing mood," Lizette growled. From her crouched position, Lizette wiped her dagger clean on a leaf. She twirled the blade in her hand and started to slide it back into its sheath at her waist.

A crackling noise behind her caused Lizette to whirl. Instinctively, she reacted, whipping the dagger towards the source of the sound.

Rin sidestepped the fast moving blade, snatching the dagger out of the air.

Lizette slowly rose to her feet. "Pretty fast, Takan."

Rin looked at the blade in his hand, at the thin line of blood the sharp edge had slit into his skin as he grabbed at it, then looked at Lizette. "I need you to come with me."

Lizette moved to Rin, taking the dagger from him. He made no effort to prevent her from taking the weapon back.

"I need to know what you saw in the house," Rin said. "I need to know what was on that display you saw."

Lizette frowned at him. "You chew too much

leaf, Takan? I already told you everything. I don't remember what else was on that display. I wasn't really paying that much attention to it. Had a few more important things on my mind at the time."

Rin was silent for a moment, staring at her. "The PowderKeeper will know." He gently tapped at the side of his forehead.

Lizette stared at Rin for a long moment, not believing what she had just heard. "You want a PowderKeeper to go rooting around in my head and drag some half-ass memory out for you?" Lizette reached out and patted him condescendingly on his cheek. "Sweetie, I think your blue skin is pretty damn hot, but I ain't letting no Keeper harvest my brain for you."

"The entire Takan race is in danger," Rin said.

Lizette held out her arm to him. "What color do I look to you?"

Rin stared hard at Lizette. "As you Humans would say… yellow."

WORZON HOLE - TEMPLE OF HUNAK - DAY

Joktala and Alaysia were eating a meal supplied by the Worzon. They sat before a long marble slab on rough stumps of wood that served as rudimentary chairs, the food just sitting in piles on the table as there were no plates to be had. It was a mixture of dried meats, fresh fruits, some leafy herbs. They did have drinking cups, however, and Hunak filled the goblets with juice squeezed from fipple fruits that he grew in a garden room, the brownish liquid filling the golden chalices nearly to the rim.

T'rok and the other Gatherers sat on the marble slab itself, taking up a third of the table. A similar selection of food was also piled up around them.

Joktala drank deeply, the cooling and tasty drink feeling exquisite as it eased down his healed throat.

Alaysia drank deeply as well, downing nearly half the contents at once. Neither one of them had drunk anything for quite some time. She rolled the golden chalice between her fingers, savoring the sweet taste of the beverage in her mouth.

Hunak watched them eat and drink, his tentacles completely still.

Suddenly both of Alaysia's hands started to turn a different color as she rolled the goblet back and forth between her fingers, a metallic gold seeping into her skin! It was as if the golden metal of the chalice was transferring itself into her flesh. Alaysia cried out, at first more in shock than because she was in any severe pain, and dropped the goblet, spilling the dark juice across the table. She raised her hands in front of herself, her face twisting in an agonized grimace as some pain did now begin to race across her hands, her fingers curled into claws, her knuckles tight with the strain.

Joktala grabbed her elbow just as she was about to fall, keeping her on her seat. "What is it? What's wrong?"

Alaysia gritted her teeth, fighting back the pain building inside her. "Joktala, help me."

T'rok dropped his food and hurried over to Alaysia, looking at her with alarm. He looked at the Worzon and chattered in what sounded like an angry voice. The other Gatherers remained huddled together, watching quietly.

The Worzon said nothing. He was too intent on watching Alaysia and the transformation that was taking place.

The metal flowed through Alaysia's body, moving from her hands to her arms, up to her elbows. When Joktala saw the metal creeping up her arm to where he was gripping Alaysia, he let go of her. He looked at the overturned chalice on the marble table, looked at the same metallic sheen starting to creep over Alaysia's flesh, then angrily knocked the chalice farther away from her with a swipe of his hand, sending it clattering to the floor. But it was too late to stop anything.

The metal skin continued to move up her arms, to her shoulders. The creeping coating of gold reached Alaysia's neck and continued rising up to her chin. She looked at Joktala with terrified eyes. "Joktala…"

Joktala whipped his head toward Hunak, glaring hotly at the Worzon. "Stop! Make it stop!"

The Worzon said nothing. His tentacles did not move. He just continued to stare at Alaysia.

Within moments, the transformation was complete. The entirety of Alaysia's blue flesh was now some kind of hardened shell of gold.

Joktala looked at Alaysia, tormented by his inability to help her, angered by the Worzon's lack of action. He stared at his companion with

142

disbelieving eyes. Her entire body had been transformed.

T'rok reached out with a tentative furry hand, but stopped short before he touched Alaysia's new flesh.

"Intriguing," Hunak said.

Joktala turned to see the Worzon watching them. "What's happening to her!"

The Worzon moved closer to them, still intently studying Alaysia. His tentacles moved now, hovering just inches away from Alaysia, but none of them touched her. "Your blood contains a residue of the powders used during the Great War. It affects each of you in a different way, mixing with your individual body fluids in unique ways." He moved closer to Alaysia, the tentacles a hair's breadth away from Alaysia's new golden skin but still not touching her. "It was a gift." He looked at Alaysia very intently. "A gift from me when I created you."

"A gift?" Joktala was incredulous. "That's a gift?"

Hunak looked to Joktala. "I was never able to give any of your forebears the final catalyst before I was nearly murdered by another Worzon intent on destroying me. I let the Takans free upon the world before you were truly finished."

The Worzon looked back to Alaysia. "I may not be able to create new life, but it appears I can still help it evolve."

Joktala looked at the fallen chalice, looked at the liquid spilling from its rim. He glanced over at his chalice, saw that it was empty. A cold rage filled his eyes. "You did this to her. To me. What's my gift? I turn into a bowl of stew and you eat me?"

The Worzon blinked slowly at him. "All Takans hold such a power buried deep inside them. But each of your gifts are as unique as yourselves."

Joktala looked at Alaysia, studied the effects of her transformation with a growing rage.

Alaysia looked imploringly at Hunak. "Please, stop this. You did it to me, now stop it. Change me back." Her lips appeared slightly stiffened by the metal, so her words came out awkwardly, the sounds not as clear, the pronunciation not as precise as the way she normally spoke.

"I cannot," Hunak said. "Your abilities are now yours to control."

Alaysia groaned, putting her hand to her head. The soft metallic clanging noise her hand made when it touched her head startled her and she quickly took her hand away from her head.

Joktala moved closer to her side. "Are you okay?"

Alaysia nodded, saying nothing, but then shook her head.

T'rok again chattered angrily at the Worzon. He reached out to Alaysia again and this time put his little hand comfortingly on her new golden flesh.

Joktala turned back to the Worzon, his jaw set tight. "Help her! You did this! Take her damn gift back! She doesn't want it!"

"You cannot erase a truth once it has been revealed," Hunak said.

Alaysia glared at the Worzon. "So we're still your playthings, right, Worzon?" Her words were filled with bitterness. "You nearly destroyed the world once, you'd think you'd have learned from your mistakes."

Hunak stared back at Alaysia, saying nothing. His tentacles were still, motionless at his side.

Joktala rose up and took a step towards the Worzon, his teeth clenching tight. "Let us go, damn you."

POWDERKEEPER SHOP
BORDERING HUMAN AND TAKAN
TERRITORY - NIGHT

Rin and Lizette were in the PowderKeeper's shop, standing before its owner, the same creature Lizette had visited earlier to purchase her ice daggers and fire blades. A few Gatherers were visible in the shop, working quietly, and the sounds of more of them working in the back room could be heard.

The PowderKeeper blinked very slowly at Rin. "I do not do this."

"We need your help," Rin said. He pointed to the small pile of coins on the counter. "That should be more than enough to cover your trouble."

"Coin not problem," the PowderKeeper said. "Keeper never link Takan and Human before. Keeper not know what happens."

"I'm willing to take that risk," Rin said.

The PowderKeeper looked at a dubious Lizette.

"Let's just do it," Lizette said. She turned to Rin, her jaw tightening. "Just because you saved my life, doesn't mean you fucking own it. After this, you stay the fuck away from me."

Rin nodded softly.

The PowderKeeper studied Lizette. "You come back. Bring little human girl-thing friends. Bring coin. Keeper, smart Keeper."

"Yeah, you're a damn genius," Lizette snarled at him.

The PowderKeeper looked at her angry face, her taut lips. "Ah, you show teeth to me."

"Can we get on with it?" Lizette impatiently snapped.

Quickly, without fanfare, the PowderKeeper attached a set of tendrils to Lizette's forehead and then attached a set of his tendrils to Rin's forehead. Their muscles froze, their bodies tensing nearly simultaneously, their arms and legs going rigid. And then their eyes went wide.

LIZETTE'S BRAIN

Inside Lizette's brain, a bright bolt of light careened through her gray matter. A red hot spark whipped along a neuron and then plunged inside a cluster of cells to reveal some of Lizette's memories. They were a weird menagerie of images, sometimes through Lizette's eyes, sometimes as if Lizette was watching herself through someone else's eyes.

A young Lizette, about five years old, gets struck by an old Human male, a heavy backhanded blow across her cheek. The blow knocks her to the ground and the old male kicks at her with filthy bare feet, his long toenails scratching at Lizette's arms as she tries to defend herself.

A young Lizette scrounges for food in the refuse bins of a tavern amidst a harsh storm. Her clothes are tattered, barely enough cloth to cover her. Lightning rips a jagged scar in the night sky, the bright flash illuminating the roachrats that scrounge along with her.

A young Lizette, now about nine, is raped by the old Human male who beat her. She is powerless to stop him, his grip too strong, his bulk too much to overcome.

An older Lizette, now about twelve, tries to teach herself how to fight, wielding a gnarled branch against a gang of Humans. She loses. Badly. She ends up bloodied and bruised.

An older Lizette gets raped again, this time by several Volgarians. They drool and slobber over her, passing her roughly amongst their group.

An older gaunt Lizette is once again rummaging through refuse bins looking for food. A tavern owner chases her away from his garbage, shaking his balled up fist at her, wielding an ominous blade in the other.

An older Lizette is curled into a ball, huddled alone against the side of a dilapidated barn as a storm rages in the sky above, her tears mingling with the rain that pounds down on her.

Not once was there a smile present on her face in her memories.

RIN'S BRAIN

Inside Rin's brain, the shape and contours and colors of his Takan brain were in marked contrast to Lizette's Human brain. The red hot spark whipped along his neurons and then plunged inside a cluster of his Takan brain cells to reveal some of Rin's memories. The recall of his memories was similar to Lizette's, sometimes seen through Rin's eyes and sometimes the memories played out as if being seen through the eyes of others around him.

A young Rin plays happily with his father, tossing a fipple fruit back and forth. Both smile broadly, easily, enjoying this simple game.

A young Rin learns to handle weapons with his friend, a young Joktala. They spar with wooden practice swords, grinning as they dramatically fight mock battles with each other.

Rin and Joktala, older now, laugh as they run from Teacher Nakarian as he shakes a fist at them.

An older Rin has cheerful discussions with his father long into the night. They both sit in overstuffed chairs before a burning hearth, the flames looking inviting and warm. His father absently smokes on his pipe, using it as an interjection device when he wants to make a strong point during their talks, pointing the mouthpiece at Rin when he gets excited about something.

An older Rin walks alone on a beautiful day, enjoying the sun. He looks up and smiles as the warm sun bathes his face.

RIN AND LIZETTE'S MERGED MINDS

And then the images started to twist and transform. The two sets of memories merged, and then the images seemed to reverse themselves.

A young Rin is being beaten, kicked and punched savagely all over his body as he curls up into a protective ball.

A young Lizette plays joyfully with friends, dancing and twirling in the sunlight, grinning from ear to ear with a dazzling, happy smile. She is a cute girl, full of vibrant life.

An older Rin is savagely attacked, and then brutally raped by a gang of Volgarians. They belch and grunt grotesquely as they pass Rin around amongst themselves.

An older Lizette is sitting at a fine table, eating a sumptuous meal with friends. She eats daintily, delicately, enjoying every morsel.

The memories, the images, the nightmares swirled around each other, continued to intermingle. Rin experienced a lifetime of being Lizette in a matter of moments, while Lizette experienced a lifetime of being Rin in just as short of a time.

Then, finally, the images faded as the PowderKeeper took firmer hold of the memories inside them, especially the memories of Lizette. He guided her in the direction they had sought, steering her memories toward the exterior of Jason

Alexian's home, forcing Lizette to focus on the task at hand.

Rin experienced the same memories now that the PowderKeeper had linked their minds together. The inside of Alexian's house flooded both their thoughts, and they both moved through the study, stopping at the table in the center of the room.

They stared at the diorama on the table. The memory of the diorama was hazy, indistinct at first, but then grew clearer. They saw Ashenwall, the buildings, the fence, its heavy defenses. And its location near the Crystal Falls.

The books on the shelves behind them suddenly just ignited, quickly sending towers of flames shooting up towards the ceiling, engulfing Alexian's study in a wall of fire.

With a shriek, the images vanished.

POWDERKEEPER SHOP
BORDERING HUMAN AND TAKAN
TERRITORY - NIGHT

Rin stumbled violently backward as the PowderKeeper released his tendrils, slamming hard against the wall, then sliding down it to lie on the floor.

A container on a shelf nearby tottered, then fell, but a Gatherer was there, grabbing it before it could shatter on the ground.

Rin held his hands to his head, pain obviously searing his brain.

Lizette fared better. She appeared shaken, but in no pain. She almost looked blissful as she stood looking at the PowderKeeper. She looked at the Takan on the ground to find him staring at her with wide eyes. She moved to his side and helped him to his feet. Lizette wrapped her arms around Rin, hugging him as tightly as she could.

Rin hugged her back immediately with no hesitation.

"I never knew life could be so wonderful," Lizette said softly, her voice barely above a whisper.

"I never knew life could be so terrible," Rin said, his voice just as soft.

They pulled back from the embrace to stare deeply into each other's eyes. They kissed desperately, their mouths devouring each other. They gripped each other tightly, pressing their lips firmly together, the kiss deepening, their passion obviously growing stronger and stronger.

The PowderKeeper watched curiously as Rin and Lizette tugged at each other's clothes. They were quickly naked, smothering each other with kisses, caresses, blatant fondling. Lizette's pale pink skin was in marked contrast to Rin's blue-hued flesh. Rin cupped Lizette's breast and she moaned hotly, leaning her body towards him, wanting him to touch her.

All of the Gatherers stopped what they were doing and turned their full attention on Rin and Lizette.

Lizette dropped to the floor, pulling a now naked Rin on top of her. "I… I can't help myself…"

she said in a breathless pant.

Rin was just as breathless. "I know."

They kissed passionately. Rin caressed her face as he kissed her, rubbing his fingers gently along her cheek and neck, then running his fingers through her hair.

"Are... we... compatible?" Lizette asked.

Rin nodded. He thrust forward.

Lizette gasped in a delighted moan of blissful pleasure. "Are all Takans so... big?"

Rin breathed heavily into her ear. "No. Just me."

Lizette wrapped her arms around his neck, pulling him closer. She breathed heavily. "Ohhh... Don't ever let go, Rin. Don't ever let go..." Tears flooded from Lizette's eyes. She raised her head toward Rin's ear. "Don't ever let go," she whispered.

Rin spoke softly back to her. "I won't... I can't..."

A few more Gatherers came out of the back room, curiously eyeing the activity taking place in the shop, watching the Takan and the Human make wild, desperate love on the floor of the shop. The PowderKeeper whistled at the little creatures and the Gatherers all returned to work. The PowderKeeper gathered up the coins on the counter and quietly moved into the back room.

WORZON HOLE - TEMPLE OF HUNAK - DAY

The Worzon looked at Joktala, Alaysia, T'rok, and the remaining Gatherers. They were standing beside the opening to the Worzon hole where they had entered his home. The swirling colors that marked the entrance, and now the exit, were not as pronounced as when viewing it from outside the Worzon hole, but they were still visible; the colors were more muted, less vibrant. There was nothing visible beyond the soft whirling colors but a deep blackness.

"I must caution you," Hunak said. "I once was able to control how my home moved through space. We used them as portals to travel quickly across the world. Some Worzons even used them to escape to other worlds as they fled our civil war. But that ability is gone, destroyed in the Great War. Now, my home, the Worzon hole as you call it, drifts aimlessly through space, carrying me with it. I don't know where you are going to end up or what you will find on the other side once you go through. You could find yourselves right in the middle of all those Skeletons again or you could end up in..." Hunak's voice trailed off and his tentacles drooped. "I just do not know."

"We'll take our chances," Joktala said.

Alaysia was quiet, lost in thought, her skin still a metallic gold. She stared down at her hands, turning them over to look at her golden palms, then flipping them around to stare at the golden backs.

Joktala looked at Alaysia. "Are you ready?"

Alaysia nodded without looking up.

Joktala looked to T'rok. The little Gatherer did his best mimicry of a nod, cocking his head sideways and bobbing it up and down.

Joktala took Alaysia's hand in his. Her metallic flesh was still warm to the touch. It still felt somewhat like skin, but her flesh definitely had a hardness to it, a thickness. She tightened her fingers around his and Joktala winced, distorting his body slightly as he unsuccessfully tried to ignore the pain her squeeze was causing him.

Alaysia noticed his discomfort and released her grip on him. "Sorry," she said.

Joktala wiggled his fingers. "It's okay." He gave her a soft smile.

"If I have caused you any discomfort, I am sorry," Hunak said.

Joktala turned to the Worzon. "If you're looking for forgiveness, forget it. Takans aren't good at forgiving." Joktala paused. "Oh, and you know those prayers I used to say to the Great One? Well, forget them, too. I take them all back."

Joktala grabbed hold of Alaysia, putting his fingers around her wrist, and they went through the hole together, quickly followed by the Gatherers, leaving Hunak standing alone.

HOME OF TAKAN RIN GRINTO - DAY

Rin and Lizette were lying in bed, wrapped in each other's arms. They were in Rin's bedroom, the bright sunlight giving the room a warm golden glow. His room was spartan, with just a large wooden bed, a chair, a small table. The walls were made of wood, barren of any decoration or shelving. He had no need for much anything else. For him, it was just a place to rest and sleep.

"What's happened to us, Rin? Every time I look at you, I just want to fu- make love to you," Lizette said.

Rin nodded. "I feel the same way." Suddenly, Rin licked Lizette's face, running his tongue along her cheek.

Lizette smiled at him. "What did you do that for?"

"Joktala said Human females like it when you lick them."

Lizette laughed. "Not in the face, honey. Not in the face."

Rin looked at her curiously.

"Oh, we are going to have some fun figuring each other out." She kissed Rin sweetly.

He looked at her for a long moment. "I feel like some of your memories are mine now. I feel like I'm inside you and you're inside me."

"Being inside me is just where I want you to be," Lizette said. Lizette reached down to his loins, but Rin grabbed her hand. Lizette put on a playful pout. "Can't we just stay in bed forever and further develop the understanding between Human and Takan?" she asked.

Rin shook his head. "We have to—"

Lizette interrupted him. "I know."

They both sat quietly for a moment, then spoke

together as one. "Ashenwall."

Lizette looked at Rin. "The PowderKeeper said he'd help us."

"We have to see Teacher Nakarian first," Rin said.

He turned to her and they kissed. The kiss deepened and they embraced, their bodies twirling on the bed.

BLACK WOODS - DAY

Joktala, Alaysia, T'rok, and the other Gatherers twirled in the air as they emerged from the Worzon hole because they found themselves tumbling through air, hurtling towards the ground!

T'rok grabbed for Joktala, clutching at his shirt, his eyes wide with fright. Joktala pulled the Gatherer to his chest, holding him tight. Suddenly, images flashed before Joktala's eyes, quick staccato bursts of sharp teeth, of strange monsters stalking a golden-skinned Alaysia, of Gatherers screaming. Joktala blinked his eyes rapidly, trying to rid himself of the unpleasant images.

Alaysia twisted and turned in the air, spinning her body around to see—

—a wall of water just before she slammed hard into it, the force of her fall sending her deep into the river!

Around Alaysia, the others splashed into the river, sending up huge gushes of water.

Joktala sputtered back to the surface, T'rok still

clinging tightly to him. The four remaining Gatherers bobbed to the surface as well. Joktala spun around in the water, searching frantically. "Alaysia?"

From high in the trees on the opposite riverbank downstream, several sets of eyes stared intently at the creatures struggling in the river. One of these creatures, a skimmur, moved to the end of a tree branch and stared hungrily down at the Gatherers. The skimmur was an ape-like creature with two long tails and a smooth, stone-like shell covering its abdomen. It had very sharp claws on its two hands and nasty, big teeth in its generous mouth.

Joktala noticed the skimmur in the tree in the distance but did not pay it much attention as he continued to move through the deep water. "Alaysia!" He glanced up to see the shimmering swirl of the Worzon hole drifting away from them through the sky, rising higher. Had they been much farther up away from the water, the force of their impact would have flattened all of them.

Upstream, behind Joktala, unseen by everyone in the river, a dark shape slinked through the water towards them. Then another shape started moving towards them, its movement only visible because of the slight rippling of water its motion caused.

Joktala heard a splash and whipped around in the water to look upstream, hoping to see Alaysia. But he did not. Instead, he saw—

—two krokors moving towards him, the ridges in their backs causing a slight ripple in the water as they moved. They swam just below the surface, remaining invisible but for the slight disturbance of the water that their motion caused. One of the krokors raised its eye stalks above the water's surface and stared malevolently at Joktala. Krokors were reptilian-like water dwellers with wide snouts and long, thin bodies covered with river-mud-brown hides. Their eyes could detach from their sockets and rise like periscopes to view what was going on above the water. They had no legs nor feet, so they were pure water dwellers, living out their lives entirely in the river.

The four remaining Gatherers squealed in fear at the sight of the eye stalks and began clawing their way through the water, desperate to get to shore, but the feeble movements of their small arms flailing wildly in the water did not give them much momentum.

One of the krokors broke off from the other and began moving towards the floundering Gatherers. It weaved its tail through the water with growing intensity, increasing its speed.

Downstream, up in the trees, two of the skimmurs wrapped their tails around a branch and began spinning rapidly, twirling their bodies around and around the branch, building up an incredible speed. They screeched wildly as they whipped their bodies in faster and faster loops, whipping round and round the branch, gaining momentum.

Joktala swam frantically for shore, T'rok clinging to his back.

The krokors were closer now. Real close. One krokor closed in on the group of other Gatherers as they flopped about in the water, and the other krokor closed in on Joktala and T'rok.

Joktala looked up into the trees to see one of the swinging skimmurs let go of its tail-grip on the tree branch. The skimmur whipped toward the water and hit the river on its stone belly, then bounced, skimming across the surface towards him. Its two tails weaved wildly through the air as it glide-bounced along the river.

The second skimmur did the same, releasing its grip on the tree branch, launching itself towards the river like a rock slung out of a slingshot. A third skimmur launched itself towards the river as well. Two of the skimmurs sped towards Joktala and T'rok, skipping along the river's surface on their rock hard abdomens, while the third skimmur whipped across the water towards the Gatherers, also skipping rapidly along the river's surface.

The first krokor reached the swimming Gatherers and its jaws opened wide, scooping a screaming Gatherer into its mouth. The krokor clamped its jaws shut and vanished under the surface of the river, the Gatherer's terrified cry muffled by the krokor's closing mouth and then completely silenced as it was pulled beneath the surface of the river.

The third skimmur whipped past the remaining three Gatherers, snatching up a Gatherer with its tails as it sailed by, curling its tails tightly around the Gather's midsection with an unbreakable grip, pulling the screaming Gatherer roughly along behind it. The ensnared Gatherer bounced roughly against the water as the skimmur dragged it behind it, the Gatherer's cry quickly turning into choking gasps, then into silence.

The river shallowed and Joktala realized he could stand. He pushed himself through the water, moving as fast as he could through the liquid. He chanced a quick glance over his shoulder and saw—

—a skimmur right on his heels, bouncing across the water, whipping its two tails towards him! One tail wrapped around Joktala's left arm, the other around his left leg as the skimmur slid past him. The skimmur unfolded its own legs and planted them into the riverbank, stopping its momentum as it reached the shore. It whipped its tails back, bringing Joktala up and over its body, slamming the Takan to the sandy ground that lined the riverbank.

Joktala grunted hard as his body was slammed into the ground. Luckily for him, the sand was soft and gave way so the impact of the blow was not as extreme had he been slammed into hard ground.

T'rok had leaped from Joktala's back as the skimmur slammed the Takan down on the shore. The little Gatherer landed safely in the shallow water near the shore—

—but only narrowly avoided the second krokor's chomping jaws! T'rok leaped away from the attacking krokor, water splashing up around him in his frantic effort to flee the striking water dweller. He made it to dry land safely and ran several feet up onto the sandy shore before risking a look back towards the river. The krokor slowly slinked back under the river, its eye stalks staying firmly focused on T'rok as it backed into the river and then disappeared under the water.

The second skimmur finished bounding across the surface of the river and planted its legs down hard as it reached the shore, joining its partner. The second skimmur wasted no time in twirling its tails around Joktala's right arm and right leg. The two skimmurs drew their tails in, raising the struggling Joktala off the ground, spread-eagling him between them. They snarled and hissed at their prey.

Joktala realized with a start that these were the monsters he had seen in his mind as he was falling from the Worzon hole moments ago. These were the horrible images that flashed through his mind, now come to life.

"No!" a voice cried out defiantly.

Joktala looked up to see—

—Alaysia standing over the dead body of the third skimmur. The skimmur's bloody guts were clutched in Alaysia's golden hand. She opened her fingers and the entrails slid from her grip. The Gatherer that the third skimmur had plucked from the river clutched Alaysia's leg, its small body trembling with fear, its drenched fur clinging tightly to its small frame making him look even smaller and more vulnerable. The other soaked Gatherers huddled near Alaysia, staying very close to her.

The two skimmurs quickly unwrapped their tails from Joktala and he dropped to the ground like a stone. The skimmurs slowly approached Alaysia, their multiple tails weaving in the air around them like angry serpents.

Alaysia glanced at the Gatherers huddled near her. "Go."

The Gatherers obeyed her strong command and

moved away from her, racing to safety deeper inland away from the approaching skimmurs. T'rok raced over to them, joining his brothers.

Suddenly, from across the river upstream, another skimmur appeared, this one larger than the other skimmurs. It screeched and raced along a tree branch, throwing its tails around the branch, winding itself round and round, building up stunning speed. It built up incredible velocity very quickly and then launched itself across the water. It hit the river on its smooth flat belly and bounced, skimming across the surface, quickly reaching the other side.

The larger skimmur hit the riverbank running and charged right at Alaysia, snapping its tails at her like whips. One of the tails raked across Alaysia's face and she cried out in surprise, turning away. She raised a hand to her face, but found no blood staining her fingers. She lifted cold eyes to the skimmur and her jaw tightened. The attacking skimmur seemed to be startled for a moment at the ineffectiveness of its blow, and Alaysia struck, slamming her golden fist into its head. The skimmur's skull cracked and the beast went down. It did not move; its tails lay motionless in the sand with nary a twitch coming from the lifeless appendages.

Joktala stared in awe at Alaysia. "Wow."

The two remaining skimmurs approached Alaysia cautiously, circling her, their tails whipping wildly about them. Suddenly, a flurry of rocks hit one of the skimmurs and Joktala turned to see the Gatherers scooping up stones and throwing them as fast as they could at the skimmur. T'rok was leading the strike, standing slightly in front of the other Gatherers, a rock clutched tightly in his little furry hand. The Gatherers screamed at the skimmur, chittering angrily, continuing to pelt it with rocks. The skimmur hissed at them and charged for them, its two tails whipping about it in a wild frenzy of motion.

T'rok ran into the river, throwing a rock at the skimmur as he ran. The stone hit the skimmur square in the face. The skimmur ran for T'rok, moving into the water. Then, the water erupted as the unfed krokor exploded out from beneath the river! T'rok dove away as the krokor clamped its jaw around the skimmur's leg. A tremendous battle ensued as the skimmur struggled to fight free of the krokor's deadly grip, whipping its tails at the krokor's eyes, but the krokor held on, victoriously dragging the skimmur under the water.

The remaining skimmur approached Alaysia cautiously. Its tails weaved about in the air, snapping and crackling like whips as they slithered spasmodically through the air like possessed serpents.

Joktala turned back to look at Alaysia and his eyes went wide. "Alaysia!"

"Get out of here, Joktala," Alaysia said, her tone commanding and very self-assured. "Take the Gatherers. I'll take care of this."

"Look at your hands!" Joktala shouted at her.

Alaysia frowned. "What?"

"Look at your hands! Your skin!"

Alaysia glanced down at her hands. Her blue-skinned hands. The metallic gold sheen that had temporarily been her new skin was now gone, replaced by the blue of her original color. Her power, her so-called gift from Hunak the Worzon, had worn off. Alaysia looked up at Joktala and she was now afraid. Very afraid. Any confidence she had been feeling completely drained from her in a matter of seconds. "Joktala?"

Joktala charged the skimmur, leaping at its back with his feet thrust forward. He hit the skimmur hard, knocking it forward. The skimmur's tails immediately whipped towards him. Joktala rolled out of the way as one of the tails snapped sharply towards him and the lashing weapon hit the ground with a loud crack.

T'rok leaped at the skimmur, throwing a rock in its face as he jumped by. The skimmur's second tail whipped around at T'rok but he scampered away unscathed.

Joktala took advantage of the distraction and dove for the skimmur's first tail, grabbing it tightly, refusing to let go as it bucked wildly. He moved quickly towards the skimmur and wrapped its own tail around its neck, pulling it tight, choking the creature. The Gatherers all grabbed the second tail and held it tight, biting it with their tiny teeth as it whipped them wildly about.

Finally, after a desperate surge of strength, his muscles bulging with the effort, the muscles in his face tightening with the strain, Joktala pulled the tail tighter, strangling the life out of the skimmur. Joktala, panting heavily from the strain and effort it took to kill the beast, released his grip on the skimmur and stepped away from the creature. The skimmur dropped lifelessly to the ground.

Joktala quickly moved to Alaysia, catching her in his arms just as she was about to collapse. "Are you all right?"

Alaysia nodded. "Just let me lie down."

He hugged her tightly to him and bathed her blue-hued cheeks with kisses. "You were amazing," he said, then gently eased her to the ground. He moved down to the sand with her and kept her head cradled in his lap, stroking her hair as he sat with her.

"Hey, Joktala…" Alaysia said, her voice weak.

"What?"

"Where are we?"

Joktala looked up to glance around the area. Towering black-trunked trees flanked the river. He took a quick look behind him and saw more coal-black trees stretching off into the distance. "Some pocket of Black Woods, but I don't know if it's the same one. I don't really know where we are."

T'rok came up to them. The other surviving Gatherers stayed close to T'rok's side, but remained slightly aloof. He reached into his pouch and pulled out a sweet leaf. The leaf was a little soggy, but still relatively in good shape. He held it towards Alaysia.

She smiled weakly at T'rok, but declined his offer with a weak wave of her hand. She noticed the other Gatherers, then looked back to Joktala. "Where are the others?"

Joktala slowly shook his head. "Some of them didn't make it."

Alaysia looked back to T'rok. "I'm sorry," she

said. She reached out a hand to him and T'rok gently squeezed one of her fingers. Alaysia looked back to Joktala. An immense weariness came over her face. "Let's go home now."

"Yeah, let's." He smiled gently at her and brushed some of her hair away from her face. "We'll bring the Gatherers back to the Keeper, then go home and sleep for two moons."

HOME OF TEACHER NAKARIAN - NIGHT

Rin and Lizette stood before Nakarian inside his living room.

Nakarian eyed them curiously, but said nothing; Rin and his Human companion stood very close to each other, clinging to each other's arms.

"You were right, Teacher," Rin said. "I know where Ashenwall is now. We need your help. We have to rally the Clans and stop them."

"I *have* rallied the Clans, Rin," Nakarian said.

Fraka Intoki, the leader of one of the Takan Clans, stepped into the living room from a back room. "But we're here to stop *you*," Fraka said. Fraka was missing two fingers on his left hand from a hunting accident in his youth. His skin was of a lighter-hue than Rin's, marking him as coming from what others called the "Pale" Clan.

Fraka was followed by Trexil Sleestaka, another Clan leader, part of Joktala's Clan. Trexil had shaved all of his hair off his head and he had a habit of constantly rubbing his hand over his bald scalp.

Rin stared with shocked eyes at the Takan leaders. They were both clearly well on in years, their flesh just starting to wrinkle which was a true sign of old age for a Takan. "Stop me? From what?"

"From destroying a fragile peace that has lasted for twenty seasons," Fraka said.

"They're going to turn us all into slaves! Into breeding stock!" Rin said vehemently. He stepped forward towards the Takan leaders, moving slightly away from Lizette, his fists clenching.

"You exaggerate, Rin Grinto," Trexil said. He rubbed his fingers over his scalp and yawned an exaggerated yawn. "You are as tiresome as your mother."

Lizette stepped forward, returning tightly to Rin's side. "No, he doesn't! I've seen it. We both heard them talk about it. I know what they're planning!"

Fraka turned cold eyes to Lizette. "A Human's opinion has no meaning to us."

Rin stared at the Takan leaders with disbelief. He looked to Nakarian for some kind of support, but his former Teacher stood side-by-side with the Takan leaders. Rin's face filled with disgust as he turned back to Trexil and Fraka. "Alexian was telling the truth. You do know about the bodies. You know the Volgarians have been taking them from our graves."

Fraka nodded. "Yes, Rin, we know. It's the price we have decided to pay to keep the peace. To prevent the Volgarians from waging war with us."

"Our dead keep us alive," Trexil said.

"This is madness!" Rin exclaimed. "And what happens now that our graves are empty?" Rin asked. "Do you give them our criminals? Our outcasts?"

Fraka and Trexil exchanged glances.

Rin's eyes narrowed. "It's not a price I'm willing to pay."

Trexil looked at Rin with a stern expression. "You have no choice."

Rin snarled. "Oh, don't I?"

"Rin, listen to them," Nakarian said. "It's the only way to prevent a war. We can't win against the Volgarians. They outnumber us four to one, perhaps more."

Rin looked hard at Nakarian, his eyes squinted, his jaw set tight. "For a Teacher, you're pretty fucking stupid."

Nakarian said nothing.

Rin turned to Lizette, grabbing her hand. "Let's go. It stinks like fear in here." Rin and Lizette turned to leave—

—but three Takan males were now standing in the doorway, blocking their exit.

Trexil looked at Rin as Rin and Lizette turned back to face the Council members, sadly shaking his head. He rubbed at his bald head. "You've got your mother's blood in you, Rin Grinto. She protested, too. She was going to expose the truth, but luckily we stopped her in time."

"Where is she?" Rin demanded.

Fraka looked at Rin. "Let's just say she is now part of the solution."

Rin glanced at Lizette and she met his gaze,

their eyes locking for a brief, but intense moment. Moving quickly, Rin grabbed a water glass from a nearby table and hurled its contents into the air, the liquid shooting out of the glass in a straight stream. Lizette dipped into her pocket and threw a handful of brown powder over the streaming water. The powders reacted with the water immediately and the water solidified instantly, forming a solid staff of hardened minerals. Rin grabbed his new weapon out of the air and spun it quickly around his body, striking one of the Takan guards across his cheek with a violent blow that sent his body spinning, the force of the strike dropping the guard to his knees. Rin continued on the attack, quickly chopping at the knees of one of the guards, toppling him to the ground.

Lizette shoved Fraka into Nakarian and Trexil, throwing her shoulder into his chest, pushing roughly against him, taking the three of them out of the fight for a moment. She whirled on the remaining Takan guard, punching and kicking with a savage ferocity, unleashing her years of training on the streets, letting her survival instincts guide her actions.

None of the guards expected such a quick and violent reaction like this so Rin and Lizette were able to clear an opening to the doorway, then escape into the night.

STREET IN FALLING STREAM - DAY

Rin and Lizette moved quickly through the streets, staying close to each other, avoiding as many other Takans as they could. Rin clutched his newly created staff in his hand. They turned sharply around a corner and—

—crashed into two other Takans walking as quickly as they were. One of the Takans fell on top of Rin and he found himself staring up at a familiar face. "Alaysia." Rin lowered his raised staff, glad that he hadn't finished delivering the blow he had intended to unleash on what he had thought had been an attacker.

"Rin," Alaysia said.

Suddenly, Lizette yanked Alaysia off of Rin and spun her around to glare hotly at her. "That was a damn shitty thing you did to me! Leaving me like that!"

Alaysia frowned, confused by this hostile Human female.

Lizette faltered, her face filling with confusion. "To Rin," she said. "To Rin. That was a shitty... thing to do... to Rin..." Lizette backed away from Alaysia. She looked down at Rin, her eyes filled with confusion and fear.

Rin quickly got to his feet and went to Lizette. "You okay?"

Lizette nodded her head. "Yeah." Then she shook her head. "No." She was quiet for a moment. "That was fucking weird. For a second, I was you. I'm me now. I think..."

Black Woods

"Hey, Rin Grinto. Told you I'd show you a good time."

Rin turned away from Lizette and saw Joktala grinning at him. Rin just stared at his friend for a quiet moment, but the surprise at seeing his dead friend did not last long; it quickly turned into pure joy and a huge grin burst onto his lips. "Somehow I knew I'd see you again. No Volgarian will ever get the best of you."

"Takans die hard," Joktala said.

Rin nodded softly. "Takans die hard."

Rin stepped towards Joktala and wrapped him in a tight embrace. The two friends clung to each other for a moment before they separated and smiled at each other.

T'rok chattered at their feet. Rin glanced down at the Gatherer, then back up to Joktala, cocking his head curiously.

"I can't seem to get rid of him," Joktala said and shrugged.

T'rok chattered something unintelligible, but he was clearly disgruntled by Joktala's offhanded remark. Alaysia bent down and gently patted his head.

Just then, the shaft in Rin's hand dissolved, turning back into a harmless stretch of water. The thick rod of water hung in the air for just a second, then fell downwards, splashing against the ground with a soft spluttering sound.

Joktala looked at Rin's empty hand, glanced at the wet spot of ground, then looked back up to his friend's face. They again stared at each other for a long moment. "By the Elders, do I have stories to

171

tell you!" they both said at the same time.

STREAM ON OUTSKIRTS OF FALLING
STREAM - NIGHT

Rin and Lizette were sitting next to each other near a stream at the edge of town, their bodies touching. Joktala and Alaysia were sitting across from them, T'rok at Joktala's feet. They barraged each other with quick questions and quick answers as friends caught up with the events in each other's lives.

"I didn't mean to leave you," Rin said to Joktala.

Joktala smiled. "Hey, the Volgarians were so busy trying to get you, they forgot about me."

Rin's face took on a somber tone. "They're taking our dead. All of them. Stealing them right from their graves."

"I'm sorry about your father," Joktala said. "I always liked him." He looked at Lizette. "And I'm sorry about your friend."

More questions were asked. More answers given.

"I can't believe the Clan leaders are in on it," Joktala said. "Then again, Trexil always gave me a creepy feeling."

Lizette remained close to Rin as they talked, holding on to his arm.

Joktala chewed absently on a sweet leaf. "Then we went into the Worzon hole."

Rin was incredulous. "You went into some Black Woods and into a Worzon hole? And you saw the Great One?"

Alaysia nodded. "Rin, he wasn't much to look at. Really."

"The Worzon did something to Alaysia," Joktala said. "Gave her some weird power. Made her skin turn into metal. You should have seen her fight. She was amazing." He smiled proudly at Alaysia. "And me too, I think. The Worzon gave me some weird ability. I… see things…"

Rin looked to Alaysia. "Can you control it? Can you make it happen when you want to?"

Alaysia shook her head. "I don't know."

"Rin rescued me from the Volgarians," Lizette said. She tugged him tightly against her, beaming Rin a smile.

"I think it went both ways," Rin said. "We saved each other."

"Luckily we were in the same Black Woods when we came out of the Worzon hole," Joktala said. "So we were able to find our way back."

T'rok chattered from his position near Joktala's feet.

"Okay, T'rok was able to find our way back," Joktala clarified. Joktala patted T'rok on the head and the Gatherer's furry face took on a smug, satisfied look.

"Then the PowderKeeper merged our minds somehow," Rin said. "I saw what Lizette saw. I know where Ashenwall is." He clutched at Lizette's hand. She squeezed his fingers tightly in return. "We know where it is. It's somewhere in the Black

Woods north of the Crystal Falls." Rin paused to stare earnestly at his friends. "We have to stop the Volgarians. No one else will."

"What about getting more Takans to help us? There must be others who will help us," Alaysia said.

Lizette shook her head, but Rin was the one who spoke. "We don't know who we can trust." He looked at the others. "We're on our own."

Joktala thought for a long moment. "I'll need a new bow."

CRYSTAL FALLS - NIGHT

The group reached the Crystal Falls, a shimmering cascade of tumbling water surrounded by outcroppings of scintillating, sparkling minerals. The water made a soothing sound as it bounced off the shiny rocks in a rhythmic pattern.

Each of them carried numerous weapons and pouches filled with various powders; Joktala and Alaysia carried small bags over their shoulders filled with additional weapons. Alaysia and Lizette also carried torches. Joktala had a new bow strung across his shoulder, along with a quiver full of arrows strapped to his back. Rin had several sheathed knives strapped to his body. T'rok had numerous pouches attached to a small belt he wore; he was the only Gatherer with them on this dangerous mission.

"There it is," Rin said. Just beyond the falls, a

dark pocket of Black Woods awaited them. Their trunks seemed darker, blacker than ever, but Rin knew that wasn't possible. It was just his nervousness darkening his thoughts. The flowing sound of the falling water nearby seemed to take on a darker tone, a pounding, pulsing noise, the longer Rin stared at the dark pocket of Black Woods that awaited them.

Suddenly, Joktala winced and took a staggered step backwards, nearly tripping over his own feet. He put his hand to his head, his face twisted in a grimace. Images flashed across his vision — a deformed Volgarian — enormous undulating tentacles — a massive shadow of some huge creature — a tremendous explosion.

Concern flooded into Alaysia's face as she noticed Joktala's obvious distress. "What is it? What happened?"

T'rok looked up at Joktala with a worried expression.

"Damn that Worzon…" Joktala muttered. "I saw… something big…"

"What was it?" Rin asked.

"A big… thing…" Joktala said. "I don't know what it was." Joktala straightened, shaking his head as if trying to dislodge the visions that had been thrust into his mind.

"Are you all right?" Alaysia asked. She put a gentle hand on his shoulder.

"Forget it," Joktala said. He closed his eyes and shook his head quickly from side to side again. "It's gone. They're gone." He opened his eyes and looked at his companions; his yellow eyes gleamed.

"Let's go."

They moved towards the Black Woods.

*****

Rin, Lizette, Joktala, Alaysia, and T'rok reached the edge of the Black Woods and stopped. They stood at the edge of the thick growth of dark, eerie trees for a long moment, the realization of what they were about to do starting to sink in deep. The night around them was eerily quiet. The sound of the falls behind them seemed to have just stopped. as if their close proximity to the Black Woods was blocking any noises from reaching them. Joktala adjusted his weapons bag, moving it to a different place on his shoulder. They all exchanged wordless glances and plunged inside the thick growth of dark trees.

The Black Woods swallowed them up.

BLACK WOODS - NIGHT

Rin took a few steps into the Black Woods and stopped, taking in his surroundings. As was usual for the interior of a growth of Black Woods, the trees seemed to glow with their own bizarre light. But in this pocket of Black Woods, a low fog covered the ground, its white wispy fingers swirling around their legs. T'rok was nearly invisible in the haze at times when the eddying movements of the low white fog swirled about him.

The flora that blanketed much of the forest floor looked different as well from the flora that had been visible in the pocket of Black Woods that Joktala and Alaysia had entered earlier. The flora that surrounded them now had sharper-edged leaves, and large thorns protected many of the plants. Strange sounds rang out in the distance, one sound echoing like a mixture of a mulger cry and a skimmur screech.

A few yards away, Rin saw a giant roachrat, the scavenging creature the size of a big dog, slither through the dark trees. "This doesn't look like what you described to us," Rin said, turning to look at Joktala.

"Hunak said each pocket of Black Woods would hold its own secrets," Joktala said. "They're all going to be different." Joktala glanced around the area. "It seems darker in these woods, so I'm glad we brought the torches."

Lizette clutched at Rin's arm, holding the burning torch high in her other hand. "Creepy, huh?"

Rin nodded. "Yeah."

They all moved slowly, heading deeper into the woods, the undergrowth crunching and crackling underfoot as they walked no matter how cautiously and gingerly they stepped.

"I can feel my feet tingling through my boots," Rin said as he glanced down at the ground.

Joktala nodded. "Teacher told us the truth about that at least. The Worzon told us the ground is saturated with the residue of magic from the Alchemy Wars. It's what makes the Black Woods what they are."

"It's also poisonous to the Worzons now," Alaysia added. "The land and the air. That's why none of them can ever come out of their Worzon holes anymore."

Lizette clutched Rin's hand in hers, squeezing it tight as they moved through the strange new world they have discovered. They continued to move through the dark woods in silence. The fog slowly started to thin as they moved deeper and deeper into the thick of the black-trunked trees.

Alaysia saw Lizette and Rin holding hands and she smiled a soft smile, wistfully sad yet happy all at the same time. She reached out and grabbed Joktala's hand. He looked over to her, and glanced down at their joined hands. He squeezed her hand reassuringly back. He looked back up at her and the reddish-orange light coming from the burning torch in her hand flickered across her beautiful face, revealing her soft smile.

T'rok saw a bright white flower growing near the thick roots of a coal-black tree and excitedly plucked it, adding it to his pouch.

They continued on, walking in silence for a while.

The group finally spotted a clearing in the distance, noticeable due to the lack of trees towering into the sky ahead.

"Put the torches out," Rin cautioned.

Alaysia and Lizette doused the flames, rolling the torches in the dirt to extinguish the fires.

They continued slowly forward and then stopped behind a thick row of bushes, careful to avoid the sharp spikes that jutted out from their branches. They peered through the gaps in the leaves, seeing—

—Ashenwall.

And it was, indeed, a formidable fortress. Or would be once it was finished. From the look of several unfinished buildings, it was obvious the compound was still under construction. Groups of Volgarians clustered around the unfinished structures, working on various parts of the buildings, wielding saws and hammers or other building tools. The light from the two moons hanging high in the night sky shined down on the fortress, their light no longer blocked by the presence of the thick trees. Torches also burned everywhere around the fortress, throwing bright pockets of light throughout the entire fortress area. Some sections were interspersed with areas of deep shadows where the torch lights didn't reach or where the walls of buildings blocked the moons' lights.

A large wooden fence surrounded the entire compound. Joktala notice a slithering motion along the fence and frowned, his face wrinkling in disgust. "Vine snakes." Vine snakes writhed and hissed amongst the wooden pickets of the fence, forming a second layer of defense filled with poisonous barbed tails and poisonous sharp fangs. They slithered along the fence, also acting as sentries as they moved, their long forked tongues flicking in and out of their mouths as they weaved around the pickets, tasting the air for any foreign scents that didn't belong. There seemed to be hundreds of them, covering every visible patch of fencing with their slithering bodies. "We'll never be able to get past those," Joktala said.

From their vantage point, the group could see two guard towers under construction nearby. Both Volgarians and Humans walked the grounds, sometimes very visible in the light cast by the moons or the torches, sometimes just barely visible as dark shapes moving amongst the moon shadows. Most of them seemed busy with the construction proceeding inside the compound, but a few Volgarians seemed to be on patrol duty as they paced the grounds in measured steps.

Just then, a mulger-driven cart overflowing with bags of sweet leaves turned into the compound, disappearing into its interior through the southern gate. For a brief moment, they saw a flash of a robed driver leading the cart.

"Look at me," Lizette said. She pointed to Rin. "Look at you." She pointed to the fortress. "Look at that. You're crazy."

Rin looked at Lizette curiously.

Lizette tapped her head. "Hey, I should know."

"You expect the four of us to stop that?" Joktala asked.

T'rok chattered loudly. Joktala glanced at him, then back to Rin. "You expect the four and a quarter of us to stop that?"

"What other choice do we have?" Rin asked.

Alaysia pointed to a large structure off to their right. "Look."

The others followed her gaze, seeing several Volgarians leading bound Takans into the building.

"How are we supposed to get in there?" Joktala asked.

Lizette grabbed Rin's hand. "Leave that to us. I have an idea."

"You do?" Rin asked.

Lizette looked at him knowingly.

Rin grinned back at her. "Yes, you do."

ASHENWALL - SOUTHERN GATE - NIGHT

Lizette led Rin by a leash around his neck. She wore leather gloves over her hands, one gloved hand tugging on the leash as they walked. Rin's arms were tied in front of him, bound by a rope that was wrapped around his wrists. Lizette stopped at the open entrance to the southern gate.

A Volgarian guard hurried over to them, stopping in front of Lizette. The guard was dressed in a drab green tunic and dull brown breeches, a sword strapped to his waist. His lips curled into an unpleasant snarl as his beefy hand went to the hilt of his sword. "What are you doing here, Human?" His mouth was pockmarked with open sores and he had a bloodshot left eye.

"Are you as blind as you are ugly?" Lizette said. "I've brought you a Takaṇ. I want my reward."

The Volgarian frowned. "Reward? What reward?"

"Don't they tell you anything?" Lizette exhaled with exaggerated annoyance. "Every Takan head is worth twenty coin," Lizette said.

A second Volgarian guard joined the first. He was dressed similarly to the first guard, wearing a uniform of drab green and dull brown that all the guards were wearing. He also had a sword scabbard strapped about his waist, as well as a curved dagger thrust behind his belt on the opposite side of his sword. "What's going on here?" He glared at Lizette. "Who are you?" He looked over at Rin and made an unpleasant face.

Rin kept his expression even, remaining calm.

The second Volgarian looked back to Lizette. "What are you doing with this blueback filth?"

"I've brought you a Takan," Lizette said. She stiffened her hips, standing defiantly before them. "I want my twenty coin."

The second Volgarian guard scowled at her. He belched obscenely in her face. "We don't offer any rewards for Takans. What are you doing here?"

Lizette waved her hand slowly in front of her face, as if daintily removing the stench of the Volgarian's belch away from her nose. "Look, your stankiness, there must be some mistake here," Lizette said. "The word is that you Volgarians are offering twenty coin for every Takan brought to Ashenwall. Well, here I am. And I want my coin or I walk and take the Takan with me."

"I'm afraid you'll do no such thing."

Lizette and Rin turned to see a large Volgarian striding towards them, the owner of the deeply booming voice that just threatened them. He was a tall brute with dark eyes and a dark, weathered face, his flesh deeply purple and blue. His nose was enormous, bulbous and knobby, far too large even for his big head. He also wore what appeared to be a uniform of some sort, something akin to what the Volgarian guards were wearing, but with more ornately elaborate stitching. He had a commanding presence, clearly of some higher authority than the two Volgarian guards. He went by the name of Gengala Kahl.

*****

Joktala tensed as he saw the big Volgarian standing before his friends. He grabbed at his bow, his hand tightening around the curved shaft. Then, a sudden burst of fear crossed Joktala's face and it was clear that another vision was flashing through his mind. For a brief moment, more images flashed by inside his head — Alaysia falling to the ground — Rin getting stabbed with a weapon — T'rok looking up in fear and thrusting his little furry hands up into the air as a dark shadow crossed over his face — Rocks crashing to the ground.

Joktala rubbed his eyes. A sheen of sweat lined his brow. His body trembled for a moment as the final images from the vision vanished from his mind.

T'rok patted Joktala's leg reassuringly.

Joktala looked down at T'rok. "Go home, T'rok. You're just going to get in the way."

T'rok did not move.

The anger rose in Joktala's tone. "Get out of here you stupid furry animal!"

Joktala kicked at T'rok, pushing him away. "I don't want you here! Leave me alone!"

"Joktala, what are you doing?" Alaysia cried out, alarm in her voice.

"I don't want this damn little beast near me!" Joktala snapped. He glared down at T'rok. "Go or I'll kill you!" Joktala knocked an arrow and pointed it right at T'rok's chest. "Go!"

T'rok looked up at Joktala, a sadness filling his big eyes, the unexpected rejection pushing his mouth down into a dejected frown. He lowered his head and scampered away.

"What did you do that for, you jreck!" Alaysia said, chiding Joktala with a sharp smack to his arm. "What did he do to you? We might need the powders he was carrying."

Joktala looked at Alaysia, lowering his bow, a sobering darkness entering his eyes. "One of us isn't going to come back from this. I didn't want it to be him. He's had enough pain in his life already."

Alaysia was quiet for a moment, studying Joktala. "Who? Who won't come back?"

"One of us," Joktala said. "That's all I know. Maybe me. Maybe you."

Alaysia was again quiet, looking at him. "Then why didn't you send me away?" Alaysia asked, her voice soft.

Joktala smiled at her and kissed her. "Because now you, as Lizette would say, are a bad ass. You can take care of yourself." He reached out and took her hand, squeezing it reassuringly. "And because I need you to protect me."

Alaysia squeezed his hand back. She leaned in and gave him a kiss.

*****

Gengala Kahl smiled pleasantly at Lizette, at least as much as a Volgarian could show pleasantry in his sourpuss face. "You are obviously full of shit. There is no offer of reward. There never has been, nor will there ever be one." He paused, put a finger to one side of his bulbous nose to close one of his nostrils, and blew out a nose-full of snot near Lizette's feet. "So the question remains, Human. What are you doing here?"

"Well, there must be some mistake," Lizette said. She took a slight sidestep away from the grotesque blob of nasal discharge near her boots. "Because that's all everyone is talking about. Everybody's out hunting Takans. You should expect plenty of visitors any day now."

Kahl frowned at Lizette. There was no hint of any amused pleasantry left in his face.

"Are you running this place?" Lizette asked.

Kahl answered immediately, standing taller with a prideful, arrogant straightening of his back. "Yes."

"Good," Lizette said. She released her hold on Rin's leash.

Suddenly, Rin grabbed the ropes binding his wrists. He crushed the tiny vial he had been holding in his hand and smeared the powder mixture along the length of the rope. The rope grew thicker and solidified, forming a barbed whip at one end comprised of a dozen razor-sharp tips. Rin swung his deadly new weapon at Kahl with a sharp snap of his wrist and the whip whistled through the air, cracking loudly as it reached supersonic speed, the bladed ends ripping through Kahl's shirt, shredding the flesh on his chest, the tips slicing deep. Kahl screeched in pain and clutched at the ragged rips in his upper torso.

Lizette quickly took care of the first Volgarian guard with her freshly created fire blade, slashing the burning blade across his throat before he had a chance to react.

Rin cracked the rope whip again, this time sending razor-sharp tips slashing across Kahl's face and neck, ripping gashing holes through his throat. The Volgarian commander was dead before he hit the ground.

The second Volgarian guard went for the dagger in his belt, his gaze intent on Lizette, but an arrow suddenly appeared in the guard's throat and he dropped like a stone, the force of the penetrating arrow thrusting him backwards.

Rin turned to see—

—Joktala and Alaysia charging forward through the open gate, Joktala knocking another arrow in his bow as he ran. They quickly reached Rin and Lizette.

"Okay, we're in," Joktala said. He glanced at the burning weapon in Lizette's hand. "Sweet blade." He looked back to Rin, eyeing the bloodied tips of the whip. "A whip?"

Rin shrugged. "I used to practice with one when we were training mulgers."

Alaysia pointed to the leash still wrapped around Rin's neck. "Are you going to keep that on? I mean, it does look good on you."

Lizette smiled at Alaysia. "Right?"

Rin frowned, looking a little sheepish. He quickly removed the leash from his neck and tossed it into a deep pool of shadow nearby.

Joktala glanced at a structure to their right. "There's a patrol heading this way but they won't round that building for a while. But we still need to move." He glanced up at the nearby guard tower that was half built; it was still under construction so no one was manning it yet. One of the Volgarian and Human construction crews was working on a different building in the far distance, so for now there were no workers or other guards nearby.

"Where's the Gatherer?" Rin asked. He quickly bent down to grab a short sword from one of the dead Volgarians and slid it into place on the side of his waist, putting the weapon behind his belt.

"I sent him home," Joktala said.

Rin looked at Joktala quietly for a moment, then gave a quick approving nod.

*****

Rin and the others finished pulling the bodies of their dead enemies behind a building, moving several crates in front of the corpses. Rin's whip was curled into tight loops and stuck into his belt. Lizette's fire blade shimmered with flame and crackled softly. They all remained ducked behind the crates, keeping hidden as best they could. Lizette tucked the fire blade down near the ground, doing her best to try and keep its glow hidden.

Joktala turned to Rin. "Now what?" He quickly

looked down to see Lizette's blade burning right near him. "That is fucking hot." He shifted slightly away from Lizette and her fire blade.

Alaysia answered Joktala's question. "We have to save the prisoners." She looked over to a nearby building that was long and narrow with a low roof, adjusting her weapons bag on her shoulder as she turned. "That could be some kind of barracks."

"Then we burn this place to the ground," Rin said.

Joktala nodded. He looked at Lizette, glanced at the fire blade she gripped, then turned back to Rin. "Looks like you brought the right Human for that job."

They moved out from behind the crates and reached the edge of the narrow building. Rin moved for the door, but a heavy padlock barred him from gaining entrance. Lizette stayed close to Rin, sometimes touching him, always remaining within a few steps from him. "Can you melt it?" he asked her.

Lizette studied the lock. "It's pretty thick. A lot thicker than the one in Alexian's house. But, yeah, I can try." She started to raise the fire blade towards the heavy padlock.

"Wait," Alaysia said.

Alaysia grabbed a grayish-brown rock from the ground and closed her eyes, trying to absorb the stone into her skin. Nothing happened. Then, Alaysia gasped and her fingers began to turn to stone, then her hand transformed, then her arm. She cried out and dropped the rock. Only her right arm had transformed, taking on the rough texture and density of the rock; the rest of her body and flesh remained Takan blue.

"Interesting," Lizette said as she studied the gray-brown stone-flesh that now covered Alaysia's right arm.

"Now what?" Rin asked.

"It's enough," Joktala said. He looked at Alaysia and she nodded.

Alaysia moved to the padlocked door and began battering the lock with her rock fist. After a few powerful blows, the lock shattered, sending battered chunks of metal to the ground.

ASHENWALL – PRISONER COMPOUND - NIGHT

Rin and company, with weapons ready, burst into the dark building to see—

—a room filled with bunks, most of them filled with inert Takans. Other Takans were milling about, engaged in low conversations; some were playing a game of dice. Bags of sweet leaves were everywhere, some half full, some overflowing with an abundance of fresh green leaves.

The two dozen Takan prisoners suddenly stopped what they were doing and stared in silence at their rescuers. They all appeared dazed, numb, as if incapable of making any quick movements. The room was suddenly very quiet.

"I'm Rin Grinto," Rin said to the room full of Takans. "Of the Grinto Clan. We're here to get you out of this place."

The prisoners made no move towards Rin, Joktala, and the others.

"What the hell is wrong with them?" Lizette asked Rin in a hushed voice. Her blade shimmered, throwing a soft reddish light across the entire expanse of the dark room.

Joktala lowered his bow and looked at a bag filled with sweet leaves near his feet. He put his arrow back into its quiver, then bent down and picked up a leaf. The leaf had thick red veins running through it, much thicker than the veins on the leaves Joktala had been chewing. "These look like the leaves I saw in the field with all those Skeletons."

"Are they drugged out or something?" Lizette asked.

"It sure looks like it," Rin said.

"That's what those Skeletons must have been doing," Joktala said. "They're making some new strain of leaf."

"For what?" Alaysia asked. Her hand and arm were still covered in the rock-like coating where she had absorbed the rock's structure into her flesh.

Joktala shook his head. "I don't know. But I remember they did kick my ass when I chewed them. I could barely think straight." Joktala looked at the red-veined leaf and made a move to toss it back down into the bag, but then paused. He kept it and pocketed it. He glanced over to see Alaysia looking at him disapprovingly. He looked away from her.

Rin moved up to one of the dull-eyed Takan

prisoners and slapped him hard across the cheek with the back of his hand. "Wake up!" There was a disgusted anger in Rin's face, as if his patience had suddenly just evaporated. Lizette stayed close to Rin, her expression mirroring his.

The Takan prisoner blinked slowly once, then more rapidly.

"Are there other Takans here?" Rin asked, his tone sharp. "In the other buildings. Are there more Takans?"

The Takan said nothing. He slowly raised his hand to rub at his cheek.

Lizette slapped the Takan prisoner's other cheek, the force of the slap harder than what Rin had delivered. "Answer me!"

The Takan prisoner remained silent.

"There are more buildings like this one," a voice from behind them said.

Rin and Lizette turned to see a Takan prisoner step towards them. Rin studied him for a moment, saw that his eyes were bright and alert, not dull and reddened like most of the other Takan prisoners. He was about the same height as Rin, but much thinner, his time in Volgarian detention taking an obvious toll on him. "I am Niklan," he said. "I have been pretending to eat the leaf," Niklan said. "The Volgarians leave me alone if I do." He pointed to his fellow prisoners. "The others…" Niklan shook his head sadly. "The Volgarians are doing it to keep us manageable. Creating a bunch of spineless leaf addicts."

Lizette put her fire blade to a nearby bed, igniting the wood. This quickly spurred activity from the Takan prisoner lying on the bed. She rose up and scampered away from the encroaching flames.

"You really like to burn things, don't you?" Rin asked.

"Got her moving, didn't it?" Lizette said. "And yes," she added. She touched the burning blade to another bed, quickly igniting it.

The other Takan prisoners started to take notice, as if the bright flames and the billowing smoke and the growing heat were enough to push them out of their sweet leaf-induced stupor. They all hurried forward towards the door, moving towards their rescuers, their eyes suddenly much more alive and alert.

"Now are you all with us?" Rin wondered, moving his gaze from prisoner to prisoner. "We're here to end this and set you free."

"How many Volgarians do you want me to kill?" Niklan asked.

Joktala dug into his weapons bag and began distributing blades and throwing stars to the Takan prisoners, starting with Niklan.

ASHENWALL COMPOUND – NIGHT

Rin, Joktala, and the others emerged from the prisoner building.

Niklan pointed to his right. "There's another building there." He pointed to another structure slightly farther off to their right, what looked like a third barracks. "And there."

Rin pointed to the second building that Niklan had indicated, then looked to several of the newly freed Takan prisoners. Two of the Takan males and one Takan female seemed much more alert now, much more aware of their surroundings, and filled with much more righteous indignation. Rin motioned to them. "You take that one. We'll take care of the other."

One of the Takan males nodded, taking the lead for their group. He gripped his weapon tightly and motioned for several other Takans to follow him as he quickly moved off towards the other prisoner building.

Rin, Lizette, Joktala, Alaysia, Niklan, and several other Takans moved towards the nearest prison building. They rounded the corner of the second prisoner building and—

—came face to face with five Volgarians!

One of the Volgarians struck first, driving his sword into a Takan prisoner, killing him instantly. Then another Takan prisoner went down, dying under the brutal slashing dagger of another Volgarian. Niklan barely missed being skewered by a Volgarian sword, but he managed to avoid the strike by leaping to the side.

Lizette struck out with her fire blade, but one of the Volgarians swatted it away, chopping down hard on her wrist, dislodging the blade from her grip. Lizette quickly dug some powders out of her pouch, but was unsure of how to mix them, and her gloved hands would have made the process even clunkier anyway. "Ah, the hell with it." She hurled the powders into the Volgarian's eyes, blinding him. Then, she struck, slamming a gloved fist into the Volgarian's gut as he struggled to clear his vision. She drew a blade from her boot and slashed at the Volgarian, criss-crossing the blade across any area of exposed flesh she could see. She eyed her fallen fire blade and snatched it off the ground.

Alaysia slammed her rock-fist into a Volgarian, cracking his skull with one mighty blow, the force of the blow dropping him to the ground. She turned to face another Volgarian, raising her rock-fist towards him.

Joktala smiled grimly at Alaysia. "I told you you were a bad ass." There was not enough room to fire an arrow from his bow, so Joktala used his bow more as a staff, wielding it like a thin club.

Rin used his throwing knives expertly, sinking three into an approaching Volgarian with swift strikes. He drew his razor-tipped whip from his waist and lashed out at another Volgarian, raking the sharp tips across the Volgarian's throat and chest.

One of the Volgarians took flight and Joktala gave chase. He charged after the fleeing Volgarian, getting ready to fire an arrow. He raced around the corner of the building and—

—slammed right into Raker! Joktala staggered back a few steps, jarred by the unexpected wall of Volgarian flesh he just struck, but stayed on his feet. The other fleeing Volgarian continued to race away, most likely to sound a warning or get reinforcements, but there was nothing Joktala could do about that now. He had a bigger problem staring him in the face.

Raker glared heatedly at Joktala, recognition flaring in his dark eyes. "You!"

Joktala recognized the Volgarian who nearly killed him in Jason Alexian's home. "Yeah, me. But this time I smell even better." Joktala raised his wrist to Raker's face. "Nice, huh?" Wham! Joktala drove his wrist into Raker's nose, crunching bone.

Raker glared at Joktala as blood dripped from his nostrils. "Now I finish what I started."

"Joktala Sleestaka does not die today." Joktala quickly struck out with his bow and whipped the top end towards Raker, capturing his head between the bow string and the bow. Joktala yanked down sharply on the bow, whipping Raker towards the ground, the sharp motion knocking his big bulk off balance, sending the Volgarian to the ground. Joktala grabbed the bow string and pulled it back as far as he could, then let go. The bow string bit into Raker's face hard, drawing a line of blood across his flesh just below his eyes.

Raker fought back, kicking Joktala back away from him, knocking the bow out of Joktala's grip. The Volgarian got the bow off his head and threw it to the ground with a snarl.

Joktala stepped forward, driving a punch towards Raker's bleeding nose.

Raker took the blow and kept moving. He grabbed for Joktala's neck, but Joktala ducked out of the way. Then, Raker landed a stunning blow to Joktala's chin, sending him sprawling to the ground. His quiver dug into his back as he slammed into the dirt and he grimaced in pain; several of his arrows spilled out onto the ground.

The angry Volgarian towered over Joktala and drew a thick blade.

Joktala's hand went to his weapons bag, going for a throwing blade, but he couldn't reach it because the bag was pinned under his body.

Raker raised up his blade.

"Then again, maybe I do," Joktala muttered as he stared at the deadly blade Raker gripped in his hand.

Then, Rin was there, snapping his wicked whip, the barbed tips striking Raker in the arm. And then Lizette was there, diving over Joktala, slashing Raker's throat with her fire blade, cutting deep into the Volgarian! Raker dropped his blade and clutched at his throat; there was no blood because the fire blade had instantly cauterized the wound as Lizette was doing the damage. The Volgarian stared at the Takans and the Human, a stunned incredulous look flashing across his eyes before his face emptied of any expression at all. Then Raker fell dead, his charred flesh smoldering as he lay in a crumpled heap on the ground.

Joktala staggered to his feet and glanced at the smoke drifting up from Raker's neck, then looked to Lizette. "Thanks."

Lizette pointed the tip of her fire blade at him in a salute. The blade crackled and then went out, the fire fading into a thin wispy line of smoke that drifted up off the metal.

Joktala turned to Rin. "You should have left him for me. He was mine." Joktala picked his bow up of the ground and snatched at the fallen arrows, returning them to their quiver. He rubbed at his jaw where Raker had struck him.

Rin ignored his comment.

Alaysia joined them, moving to Joktala immediately as she noticed he was looking a little battered. "You okay?"

"Nothing a little leaf won't cure," Joktala said. He reached into one of his pouches at his waist and produced two sweet leaves. "You want some?" he asked Alaysia.

She shook her head.

Joktala looked down at the sweet leaves in his palm. One of the leaves had the dark red veins from the ultra-potent strain of leaf, the other was more of the normal variant he was used to. He chose the normal leaf and popped it into his mouth.

Niklan rejoined them, breathing heavily from racing up to them. "There were about twenty Takans inside. I told the others who were with us to stay with them. They're moving on to another building to free more of us."

Rin nodded. "Good."

"One of the Volgarians got away," Joktala said. "So we might have some big trouble heading our way." He looked off in the direction the Volgarian had fled. Then Joktala noticed a glow coming from the distance. His eyes filled with alarm. "By the Elders…"

"What? What is it?" Rin asked.

Joktala took off towards the source of the glow, gripping his bow tightly as he ran, bolting away from the others, racing around the corner of a nearby building, disappearing from view.

Rin looked at Alaysia questioningly.

Alaysia looked back at him, then shrugged. "He's leafed up." She turned to hurry after Joktala.

Rin, Lizette, and Niklan raced after them.

*****

Rin, Lizette, and Niklan raced up to Joktala who was staring numbly into the distance, his face bathed in a multi-colored, flowing swirl of light. "What's wrong with you?" Rin asked, looking at Joktala with a concerned expression.

Alaysia was already at Joktala's side, her eyes wide. "It's not moving," Alaysia said.

Finally, Rin turned to gaze at what was drawing their attention, seeing—

—a Worzon hole floating a few feet above the ground, its entrance marked by a rainbow swirl of light. Several beams of light seemed to penetrate into the ground, the beams coming out of the edges of the Worzon hole, as if they were spikes holding the Worzon hole in place.

Rin was awed by the sight. "A Worzon hole."

Joktala was equally awed. "An anchored Worzon hole. I didn't even know that was possible."

They were staring at the Worzon hole from a side angle, nearly perpendicular to the opening, just able to see the opening. The opening appeared to be about ten feet tall, and about as wide but they couldn't tell for sure from the angle they were looking at.

Suddenly, five Volgarians came charging out of

the hole. They raced away from Rin and the others, heading towards the sounds of a heated battle in the distance, hurrying towards the several buildings that were now going up in flames.

"Is it just me, or were all those Volgarians naked?" Lizette asked.

No one had an answer. They all stared at the Worzon hole.

Alaysia turned to Joktala. "Don't tell me. We're going in, right?"

WORZON HOLE – OUTER CHAMBER - NIGHT

Joktala and Alaysia tumbled into the Worzon hole first, quickly followed by Rin, Lizette, and Niklan. They quickly got to their feet and huddled together, studying their surroundings. Lizette stood close to Rin, their shoulders touching. They all saw that they were standing in a cavernous room, with a high domed ceiling far above.

But this Worzon hole was in marked contrast to Hunak's dwelling. There were no statues of beings lining the walls like they had seen in Hunak's home. The interior of this Worzon hole was overrun with strange plants instead; thick green vines climbed up the walls, intermingling with thinner brown vines. The ground was covered with debris and decay. Small creatures of all sorts seem to just roam randomly in the interior. Several roachrats scurried past; a few gryfwings jump-floated from vine to vine above their heads. In the distance, an animal screamed and the group whipped their heads towards the disturbing sound.

"Is this what the other Worzon hole was like?" Rin asked. He kept his voice low, barely above a whisper.

Joktala looked away from the bizarre surroundings to glance at Rin and shook his head. "Not quite."

"What is this place?" Niklan asked. He made no effort to hide the fear in his voice, and his terror was plainly visible in his face.

"Just stay close to us," Alaysia said.

Suddenly, they heard footsteps approaching from a doorway to their right. They all hurried behind a fallen pillar and hid, crouching down out of sight.

Rin lifted his head cautiously above the edge of the pillar to see—

—a naked Volgarian moving quickly past. The Volgarian's purple-blue skin looked shiny, almost wet, as if he had just emerged from some water. And his skin also looked gooey, as if he had just smeared eggs all over his body. The Volgarian hurried to the swirling portal entrance and went through, disappearing into the world outside.

Rin ducked back behind the pillar. "It was a Volgarian. It went out through the hole. It looked strange, though. All wet and slimy."

The group slowly rose from behind the pillar, but then ducked back down as another naked, slime-skinned Volgarian appeared, coming from the same direction in which the first Volgarian had approached.

Suddenly, two arrows appeared in the Volgarian's chest and he dropped to the ground without even a grunt.

Rin turned to see Joktala gripping his bow.

"Let's see what's in that room," Joktala said.

*****

Rin entered the hallway first, followed closely by Lizette, then by the others. Rin fingered his whip as he moved, but left it in place at his waist. Joktala clutched at his bow. Alaysia's hand was still covered in a layer of rock-flesh and she kept her fingers curled into a fist. Niklan stayed close to Alaysia, nervously glancing about as they moved.

They found themselves in a long, dimly lit corridor, its walls made of some smooth, marble-like material. The walls gave off a faint glow similar to the glow the dark-trunked trees gave off in the Black Woods. The corridor curved in the distance, but they saw a patch of brighter light spilling into the hallway from beyond the curve. They moved forward towards the light.

"There should be a Worzon around here somewhere," Joktala said, keeping his voice in a low whisper.

They reached the curve in the corridor and began to move around it when a shadow appeared on the wall, looming large, coming towards them. Rin held up his hand, motioning for the others to stop. He looked at the shrinking shadow, the dark outline growing smaller and thinner as whomever, or whatever, was casting the shadow moved farther away from the source of light at the end of the corridor and closer to them. Heavy footsteps could now be heard accompanying the approaching shadow. Rin glanced about them, then looked back down the hallway, back in the direction they had come, but he made no move to race back in that direction; there was nowhere for them to hide.

Then the source of the shadow revealed itself as another naked Volgarian appeared, his body shining, gleaming with goo as he walked straight at them. The Volgarian stopped as he saw them standing in the corridor. He opened his mouth to shout a warning but then an arrow appeared in his throat and the only thing that came out of his mouth was his own blood.

Joktala lowered his bow. "I hate Volgarians." He reached back into his quiver, grabbing another arrow. "Especially snot-covered naked ones." He fired a second arrow, striking the Volgarian in the chest.

The Volgarian gurgled for a few more seconds, then dropped dead to the corridor floor.

Rin stepped closer to the dead Volgarian, studying him. He bent down, moving his face nearer to the body to get a better look in the murky light of the corridor. The Volgarian's skin was covered with a thin coating of some viscous fluid, some kind of mucous-like coating. Rin glanced up, looking down the corridor in the direction their group was headed. "What are they doing in there?"

The group continued on down the corridor, moving cautiously, slowing down as they reached the end of the hallway. They stood motionless at the entrance to the room before them, their eyes wide with disbelief, their mouths opening in awe.

WORZON HOLE - CREATION CHAMBER - NIGHT

The four Takans and one Human stood before a gigantic Worzon, a Worzon ten times as wide as Hunak and even more times than that taller. It towered up nearly to the roof of the chamber that was high above, and filled up about three-quarters of the large room. Its main body had more of the appearance of a wingless insect queen than anything else. It was an amorphous, blob-like being with yellowish-white skin covering its massive bulk. From where they were standing, they couldn't see if it had any eyes or not. It had numerous tentacles just as Hunak did, some of them weaving in the air about its body, while others laid inert against its massive form. Numerous purplish-blue embryonic sacs were growing all over its enormous slug-like body, most of the sacs positioned near the wide bottom of the Worzon. The skin of these sacs was translucent, each of these external wombs with a Volgarian growing inside.

"I saw this," Joktala said. "This is what I saw in my head near the Crystal Falls." He paused. "At least we now know why we've never seen a Volgarian female before."

"What is it?" Niklan asked.

"A Worzon," Joktala said. "A big fat disgusting

Worzon making a batch of big fat disgusting Volgarians."

"It's making Volgarians?" Niklan asked.

Joktala nodded. "This Worzon is the Volgarian's creator. Or at least one of them. Look, right there." Joktala pointed to one of the womb-sacs that looked the most engorged, its purplish-blue skin stretched tight. The Volgarian inside the womb-sac was pressed tight against the wall of the sac, his arms and legs threatening to burst out at any moment. "That one looks like it's about to pop."

Rin took a hesitant step closer, seeing a reddish-colored sac suddenly appear on a different area of the Worzon's body, positioned higher up from the purplish-blue sacs that held the Volgarians. This sac was much bigger than the others, nearly twice as big. Inside this red sac, Rin saw a different form slowly taking shape, something that wasn't a Volgarian. Something with wings.

Alaysia's scream suddenly filled the chamber.

The group quickly looked towards the source of her terror to see—

—a dead Takan dangling from one of the Worzon's tentacles, the corpse curled in the Worzon's tight grip. On the ground nearby, a pile of dead Takans sat near the monster; it was just a tumbled mass of Takan corpses lying in a heap, as if the bodies had just been unceremoniously dumped on the ground like food being dumped into a trough. The Worzon wrapped another smaller tentacle around the neck of the Takan corpse and ripped its head right off. Fluid began spurting from the Takan corpse and the tentacle positioned the bleeding

Takan over a misshapen black orifice, pouring blood into the Worzon's mouth. Then, the Worzon dumped the entire corpse into its mouth. Bone-crunching, flesh-grinding noises came forth from inside the Worzon's mouth.

"By the Elders, it's feeding on us," Joktala said. He armed his bow and fired an arrow straight at the Worzon's mouth, but one of the smaller tentacles snatched the arrow out of the air before it could strike the Worzon's body and hurled the arrow to the ground.

Another dead Takan appeared in a tentacle, the body taken from the pile of Takan corpses. It was the body of a Takan that Rin clearly recognized. His face flooded with anguish. "Mother!" Rin charged the Worzon, striking out with his barbed whip, the whip snapping with a loud sound as it struck the Worzon's gelatinous mass. A red liquid oozed from the numerous gashes caused by the whip's sharp tips, but they were quickly sealed as the Worzon's yellow-white flesh filled in the cuts.

Lizette joined Rin, hacking and slashing with a fire sword she had just created with her powders, cutting deep into several tentacles that tried to grab Rin. "Let go of her!"

Joktala knocked an arrow and fired, aiming for the Worzon's beady black eyes that were now visible near the upper portion of its huge mass. Tentacles again grabbed the arrow out of the air, stopping the strike.

Alaysia punched at the Worzon's blob-like body with her rock-fist hand, but her hand just disappeared into the ooze of the Worzon's body and did no damage to the beast.

Niklan only had a small dagger, but he did his best, slashing at any tentacles that came near.

Rin continued to attack with the whip, lashing out, striking the Worzon, putting more gashes into the creature's flesh. The Worzon quickly healed every gash. Then a tentacle managed to wrap itself around the whip and the Worzon yanked it sharply out of Rin's hand. Rin immediately drew his short sword and started hacking and slashing with his blade, a manic desperation fueling his strength. "Let go of her!" Rin was close to the Worzon's massive body now, but his mother was too high to reach, the tentacle gripping her waving wildly far above him.

Lizette was at Rin's side, she too hacking and slashing. Her fire blade was doing more damage than the whip had done and she managed to sink the crackling blade deeper and deeper into the Worzon's flesh.

The Worzon made a grotesque mewling sound, as if it was moaning in pain, and lost its grip on Rin's mother, uncurling the tentacle that was wrapped around her waist. The Takan corpse dropped to the ground.

Many of the tentacles converged towards Lizette, weaving and flailing about wildly in the air. They tried to grab her, but Lizette was too quick with the fire blade, adeptly able to defend herself with quick slashes and arcing cuts.

Rin raced to his mother's side and pulled her away from the few grabbing tentacles that sought to resume the feeding process, hacking at any that came near with his sword.

Suddenly, all of the purplish-blue sacs on the massive Worzon began to pulsate and throb wildly. The fluids pumping through the purplish-blue membranes quickly trickled down to nothing. The Worzon's waving, darting tentacles suddenly dropped to lay motionless against the mammoth beast.

Rin and the others watched curiously, expecting something but just not quite sure what. Joktala had an arrow knocked, but he lowered the bow, watching, waiting.

Nothing happened.

"What's going on?" Niklan asked. "Is it dead?"

Rin took a hesitant step towards the massive Worzon.

Kaplop! Kaplop! Kaplop! Kaplop! All of the purplish-blue sacs burst wide open, their inhabitants spilling out into the room in a jumbled mass of Volgarian shapes, stunted arms and legs, distorted torsos and misshapen heads, all of them coated in thick glops of amniotic slime.

At the same time, the creature inside the red sac started to quickly take shape, forming much faster now as the Worzon pumped massive amounts of fluid into the sac. By aborting the Volgarian growths, the Worzon was able to divert its precious life-giving nutrients into other entities.

And on the other side of the Worzon, unseen by its Takan attackers, another large red sac appeared, a creature growing quickly inside this external embryonic womb as well as fluids and fleshy clumps and other bits of organic material began shooting into the sac.

Rin stared with growing disgust at a grotesque cluster of half-formed, half-shaped Volgarians lying in haphazard groupings on the floor of the chamber. Some of them were clearly dead on arrival; they were actually more of an unborn aborted mess than dead as they never reached full growth before being disgorged by their Worzon creator.

Two of the newly-born Volgarians could not even rise because their legs were so horribly disfigured that they couldn't bear the weight of their bodies. Lizette made sure they would never stand as she slashed at their throats with two deadly strikes of her fire sword.

A few of the Volgarians were nearly fully formed, and they were able to rise quickly to their feet and start to assimilate what was happening around them.

Alaysia took down a few of these disfigured Volgarians with quick, killer punches from her stone-hand. She brought her rock-fist down atop the skull of another rising Volgarian, cracking his head with one blow. The Volgarian collapsed in a heap back to the floor, his brain matter oozing out of his split skull.

Niklan moved to a Volgarian, who only had one functioning arm, as the Volgarian was starting to stand, and thrust his dagger into the Volgarian's gut several times. Niklan drew the blade out, the blade making a slurping, sucking sound as it withdrew from the brute, then thrusting it back in to a different place in the Volgarian's gut.

Joktala brought another three Volgarians down with arrows. Then, he saw one of the red sacs, saw what was taking shape within it. His face filled with urgency. "Rin, here! It's using all of its energy to make a Seeker Destroyer!" Joktala hurried towards the red sac, firing arrow after arrow at it. Tentacles snatched at his arrows, but one of them managed to get through, sinking into the red sac, making it ooze Worzon blood.

"What is it?" Rin asked as he saw large wings taking shape on the creature within the red sac, and what appeared to be the shape of a rider forming atop the creature's back.

"It's making a Seeker Destroyer!" Joktala shouted. "We have to kill it now!"

The group all converged near the bulging, throbbing red sac. Joktala fired arrow after arrow up at it, but his quiver was nearly empty and he wasn't doing enough damage; most of his arrows were still getting snatched out of the air by the Worzon's tentacles. "Alaysia, throw an exploding star at it. Do it now!"

The Seeker Destroyer continued to form within the red sac, the rider starting to take on a definitive shape, looking like a stunted Human.

Alaysia fumbled through one of their weapons bags and pulled out a sharp multi-tipped star, clutching it awkwardly with her stone-fingers. "Where's the powder?" she shouted as she rummaged through the bag with her normal hand.

Joktala fired another arrow. "In a pouch. At my waist."

Alaysia hurried over to Joktala and flipped open one of his pouches. She thrust her hand inside the pouch and came out with some blueish powder on her fingers. "The blue?"

"No, the green. Next to it. Then mix it with the orange."

Alaysia flipped open the pouch next to the pouch that contained the blue powder and was about to thrust her fingers inside when Joktala twisted his body away from her, preventing her from reaching into the pouch. "Wait!"

Alaysia frowned at him. "What?"

Joktala looked at her blue-powder-tipped fingers. "I don't know what happens if we mix those. Be careful."

Alaysia quickly wiped her fingers on her breeches, flashed her mostly-clean fingers at Joktala, then dug into the pouch and pulled out some green powder. She sprinkled the powder over the blade.

"Now some orange. Next to the green," Joktala said, speaking the words quickly, keeping his grip tight on his bow. He kept his gaze focused on the Worzon, on its weaving tentacles, on the pulsating, throbbing red sac that was continuing to expand.

Alaysia flipped open another pouch at his waist and stuck her green-powder-tipped fingers into the pouch. She grabbed a pinch of the orange powder and quickly dusted the powder over the blade. The throwing star flared for a brief second, then glowed a deep orange; lightning-shaped flashes of green light darted across its surface.

"Throw it!" Joktala urged as he fired another arrow.

"You know I can't hit—" Alaysia started to say in protest, but Joktala quickly cut her off.

"Just throw it!" Joktala said, his voice urgent, his grip tight on his bow. "You can do it."

Alaysia only hesitated for a second, then took aim and hurled the throwing star up at the pulsing red sac. The star grew, expanding as it flew, but the distance wasn't very great so it didn't expand much. Alaysia missed the red sac, but she managed to hit the Worzon's body just where the sac joined the Worzon's flesh. The star exploded, severing the red embryonic sac from the Worzon's body, splashing Worzon blood and chunks of its flesh in all directions. The red sac tumbled down the Worzon's body and hit the floor near the group with a wet splashing plop.

"Look at your fingers," Lizette said to Alaysia. She pointed her fire sword at Alaysia's hand; Niklan reared back away from the heat of Lizette's burning blade as she turned the fire sword towards Alaysia to point at her.

Alaysia glanced down to see that her Takan-flesh fingers were now glowing a deep orange and lightning-shaped flashes of green light flittered across the surface of her flesh. She looked up at Joktala with nervous eyes.

"Don't make any sudden movements," Joktala told her. "I think the quick motion activates the powders fully, so don't move." He quickly glanced about the area, stopping his gaze on a fallen Volgarian with twisted, half-formed limbs.

Alaysia stared at her glowing fingers with growing alarm, trying to keep them as still as possible.

Joktala moved to the Volgarian and grabbed at

one of his limbs, violently ripping and twisting it, tearing it away from the Volgarian's corpse with a frantic surge of strength. He quickly moved back to Alaysia and poured the blood oozing from the severed arm over Alaysia's glowing, crackling fingers. Her fingers sparked, the light flaring up as the blood hit the crackling flashes of green light that were dancing across her fingers, but they did not detonate; the blood successfully defused the powders' effects and the glow vanished from Alaysia's fingers.

Alaysia exchanged a nervous glance with Joktala, but neither of them said anything. Joktala tossed the severed Volgarian limb to the ground. Alaysia quickly brushed her blood-soaked fingers across her breeches, doing her best to wipe away any residue of powders that were left on her fingers.

"It's still moving!" Niklan shouted as he pointed at the creature squirming inside the severed red sac.

They all struck at the red sac immediately with their weapons, hitting it with a fire blade, swords, a stone fist, arrows, finally ripping the sac open and slaying the half-formed Seeker Destroyer that had been growing within before it could be born.

More large red sacs appeared, forming all around the Worzon.

"We have to stop them! If they all come out, we're finished!" Joktala shouted to the others.

Rin turned back to see that the Worzon's tentacles were active again, trying to reach his mother's body. He dug into his pouch and pulled out a large vial of a golden powder. He ran to his mother's body and spread the powder all over the corpse. "Joktala!"

Joktala saw what Rin was doing and he quickly dug into one of his own pouches, pulling out a vial of orange powder. He pulled the last arrow out of his quiver and smeared the arrow tip with the powder. A ripple of crackling light spread across the arrow tip. The PowderKeeper had told them of various combination effects the powders would have when mixed together, but he wasn't exactly certain that this was the right combination. He knocked the arrow and readied himself. Now was not the time to second-guess himself. "I don't know if this will work," he said to Rin. "But let's do it."

Rin looked down at his mother to see her eyes were open, staring up at him but not seeing him. "Goodbye, Mother. Have a peaceful Journey. You can rest now. I'll take over from here." Rin closed his mother's eyes, then pushed the body back towards the tentacles. The tentacles immediately latched onto the corpse, one tentacle gripping her torso, another gripping her legs, and raised it up towards the Worzon's mouth.

Just as the body began nearing the mouth, Joktala took careful aim.

Another tentacle started twisting the head of Rin's mother's corpse off.

Then, a horrible, ear-piercing screech filled the cavernous room. All eyes turned to see—

—a Seeker Destroyer stretching its leathery wings, its trollish rider glaring hotly at them as it descended to land on the chamber floor! It truly was a hideous monster, unlike anything they had ever seen before. The bird-like beast had a thickly scaled hide with sharp clawed fingers at each wingtip; its long beak was filled with jagged teeth. The rider, an ugly little brute who seemed to be part Human, part Takan, and part Volgarian, was melded to the bird, as if fused into the bird's back, so it had no visible legs; only the rider's upper torso, arms and head were visible. It had no hair, a pockmarked face, and flesh that was a tumultuous mixture of pink Human flesh, blue-tinged Takan flesh and purplish-black Volgarian flesh. Its tiny eyes radiated an evil, a brutal hunger that burned deep inside its black-and-red streaked orbs.

"Ki—kill—kill them—kill them all." A scratchy, but still commanding voice filled the chamber.

The Seeker Destroyer turned to see a deformed Volgarian pointing to the intruders, the head of the bird and the head of the rider turning in perfect unison.

Joktala and the others turned to the sound of the voice as well, seeing the Volgarian standing firmly on two fully developed legs. He had one stunted arm, only half-formed, but the other arm was fully developed and it pointed an unwavering finger at their group.

"Kill—kill them—kill them all," the deformed Volgarian commanded.

The Seeker Destroyer rider obeyed its master and shoved its hand into the flesh of the bird's side, sinking its fingers deeper into the very innards of the bird, pulling out a spear hewn from bone and blood and skin. The Seeker Destroyer rider hefted this horrible weapon, wrapping its bony fingers around the shaft; blood lined the entire length of this bone-flesh spear and deep crimson drops dripped off its tip. The Seeker Destroyer rider wasted no time in hurling the spear.

The spear whipped through the air, spatters of blood flying off its length as it flew, and skewered Niklan square in the chest, piercing through his breastbone and erupting out of his back. The violent force of the strike sent Niklan crashing to the floor, a thick trail of blood smearing along the ground behind his body as he skittered across the floor. He was dead before his body stopped sliding.

The others could only look on in horror. There was nothing they could do for him now.

The Seeker Destroyer rider again shoved its hand into the bird's side, pulling out another blood-soaked spear of bone. The bird creature charged forward, moving directly for Joktala, its clawed feet clacking heavily on the stone floor, the rider rearing its arm back, preparing to strike.

Then, suddenly, T'rok was there, charging the Seeker Destroyer with a small ice blade, leaping towards the monster, swinging his frozen dagger at the rider's head! The small Gatherer was cocooned within a circle of bright white light, a light that was shaped very similar to the white flower T'rok had discovered in the Black Woods.

The Seeker Destroyer rider turned towards the attacking Gatherer just in time to get a mouthful of frigid iciness! T'rok's blade slashed across the Seeker Destroyer rider's upper lip, turning its reddish-brown lip to an icy blue. T'rok leaped away from the Seeker Destroyer's spear as the large jagged tip nearly skewered him, but the spear tip bounced off the light shield that was protecting him, leaving him untouched and unharmed.

"T'rok!" Joktala shouted.

T'rok scampered away from the Seeker Destroyer, moving behind a pile of dead misshapen Volgarian abominations.

Joktala, seeing that T'rok had escaped the Seeker Destroyer's strike, whipped his head back towards the Worzon's mouth. The body of Rin's mother was halfway inside the mouth now. Joktala released the arrow. The arrow sailed towards its mark. A small tentacle reached for the arrow but a well thrown dagger by Lizette sliced through the reaching appendage. The arrow flew true, striking the corpse of Rin's mother in the chest. The powders mixed instantly and a tremendous explosion rocked the Worzon, sending chunks of its massive body flying in every direction!

The force of the explosion sent the Seeker Destroyer tumbling and both the rider and the bird screeched as the beast went end over end. It curled its wings up over the rider, trying to protect itself as best as it could as it rolled.

Everyone in the group threw their hands over their heads, doing their best to avoid the chunks of Worzon flesh and spraying geysers of blood.

Joktala raised his bow over his head, blocking a severed red sac from striking Alaysia.

A huge severed tentacle landed near Lizette and she instinctively lashed out with her fire sword, severing the tentacle into several more sections.

A red sac landed right near Rin and he launched a knife attack on it, hacking and slashing. Lizette quickly joined him, butchering the inhabitant of the sac until there was no recognizable shape left.

All of the tentacles on the Worzon quickly collapsed, falling lifeless against the Worzon's body or flopping to the ground. No more fluid gushed into the various red sacs that had started to form on the Worzon's body.

For a moment, everything was still. Several malformed Volgarians continued to moan from their positions on the floor, but the sounds they made were muted and barely distinguishable.

Joktala lowered his bow, taking in his surroundings, making sure Alaysia was all right. He saw T'rok poke his head up over the pile of malformed Volgarian bodies and he gave the little Gatherer a slight nod; the soft white glow still surrounded T'rok, his light shield still giving him some protection.

Rin reached out and squeezed Lizette's hand. She squeezed his back. Lizette's fire blade crackled, then went out; slight curling ribbons of smoke drifted up from the sword.

And then the floor started trembling beneath their feet. The walls started crumbling, just slight cracks forming at first, but the cracks quickly grew wider, quickly spread faster. Huge slabs of the ceiling plummeted towards the ground. The Worzon's home was falling apart.

"Let's go!" Joktala shouted. "I think it's dead. This whole place is going to collapse!"

Everyone converged on Joktala and they sped out of the chamber, holding their arms up as pieces of stone dropped from the ceiling all around them.

They raced through the corridor, hurrying past the dead Volgarians they had killed earlier, sprinting for the swirling circle of light that marked the only way in or out of the Worzon hole.

The walls and ceiling continued to crumble around them.

WORZON HOLE - OUTER CHAMBER - NIGHT

Rin, Lizette, Joktala, Alaysia, and T'rok charged into the cavernous outer chamber and saw a massive tangle of fallen debris and animals running madly about. The Worzon hole had been in ruins when they first entered, but now the chaos was ten times as bad.

Joktala looked up in horror to see a big section of the ceiling drop away, falling straight for T'rok. "T'rok!"

T'rok looked up at Joktala's cry and was buried under a huge pile of rubble!

"No!" Joktala raced over to the fallen rubble, frantically pulling the chunks of stone away, clearing a way towards T'rok. Then, after turning over a giant rock, Joktala froze. "T'rok."

There was no response.

"T'rok," Joktala said again. He stared down at T'rok who was still cocooned in the bright white glow, safely contained within the protective shield.

T'rok popped a sweet leaf into the Takan's gaping mouth. "Fuck you," the little Gatherer said. The glow that had surrounded T'rok faded away, his shield now gone.

Startled, Joktala spit the leaf back out. "You—"

Scraww! A thunderous screech drew Joktala's gaze back to the others. Scraww! The Seeker Destroyer was now aloft, flying through the falling stone, exploding into the outer chamber, attacking Alaysia with its deadly bone spear, snarling savagely! She raised her stone-hand and blocked the spear tip as the rider lunged at her. The horribly grotesque Seeker Destroyer rider leered with darkly evil eyes at Alaysia.

Rin knocked the creature back with an expertly thrown dagger that sunk into the rider's shoulder. But then the rider whirled on Rin with amazing speed and attacked savagely, driving its spear into Rin's left shoulder!

Lizette clutched at her left shoulder, grimacing in pain, somehow feeling the biting agony that Rin was feeling. "Rin!"

Rin went down, gritting his teeth in pain, clutching at his shoulder. The Seeker Destroyer landed near the fallen Rin, its clawed feet clacking along the floor as it moved closer. The fused rider bent close to Rin's pain-wracked face. It raised its spear and—

—got clobbered in the side of its head by a rock. The Seeker Destroyer rider looked up to see Lizette hurling another stone at it. She ignited a new fire blade, smearing a reddish powder along the length of her sword, and waved it at the monster.

"Come on, you ugly bastard. I'm here. I'm here for you."

Alaysia took advantage of Lizette's distraction and charged the Seeker Destroyer, her stone-fist raised.

But the Seeker Destroyer bird saw her charge and slammed one of its wings into Alaysia, catching her completely off guard, sending her flying over a pile of fallen debris.

"Alaysia!" Joktala cried out.

Alaysia hit the ground hard, landing near the dead Volgarian Joktala had killed earlier with his bow. The pouch of weapons she had been carrying flew off into the distance, landing amidst a pile of overgrown foliage. She began rising to her feet, then stopped, staring intently at the Volgarian body.

Suddenly, T'rok screeched nervously and grabbed at Joktala's leg, pointing into the distance. Joktala turned to see—

—the entrance to the Worzon hole was collapsing, falling in on itself, the swirling colors starting to dim, the hole starting to shrink.

Joktala looked over to Lizette and Rin. "The Worzon hole is collapsing! We have to get out of here!"

Lizette waved her fire blade back and forth before her, keeping the Seeker Destroyer at bay. "Take Rin! Get him out!"

"No!" Joktala yelled. "I'm not leaving Alaysia."

"I'll get her," Lizette said. "Now get Rin and get him out. I can't lift him."

Joktala did not move.

"Do it or I'll fucking kill you, I swear it!" Lizette snarled.

Joktala hesitated for a moment, then hooked an arm around Rin's shoulder, lifting his wounded friend to his feet. "Females…" Joktala muttered. Together, he and Rin staggered through the rubble and falling debris, hurrying as fast as they could towards the collapsing exit. A large rock crashed into the floor a few inches from them, nearly hitting Joktala, just barely missing his foot.

Then, T'rok saw the dropped weapons pouch in the rubble that Alaysia had lost. He darted back into the chamber for it, racing around the Seeker Destroyer.

Joktala shouted at the little furry animal as he raced away from them. "T'rok! No! You stupid Gatherer!" Joktala hesitated only for a moment, then continued on towards the collapsing hole. As they reached the dwindling exit, Joktala turned back to look at Lizette. The Seeker Destroyer hovered over her, the rider stabbing at her with its spear, the bird thrusting at her with its teeth-filled beak, but she was able to avoid the thrusts and struck back with her fire blade, keeping the creature focused on her.

Then, suddenly, a different sort of creature appeared from behind the rubble.

Joktala stopped, staring with transfixed eyes at—

—a transformed Alaysia, her skin now in the form of a Volgarian female.

"Destroyer!" Alaysia commanded.

The Seeker Destroyer bird and rider both

swiveled their heads towards Alaysia. They looked curiously at Alaysia, confused by her Volgarian appearance.

"Stop!" Alaysia commanded.

The Seeker Destroyer stood motionless, obeying its new master. Alaysia stepped closer, moving right up to the beast.

Joktala watched with baited breath as Alaysia reached the Seeker Destroyer and stood within a mere few feet from it.

The Seeker Destroyer rider stared at Alaysia. The bird sniffed at her.

"Now, Lizette. Now!" Alaysia shouted.

Lizette struck, swinging her fire blade at the bird, slicing through one of its wings. The bird howled in pain, writhing in agony. Alaysia reared back and delivered a stunning blow to the rider's face, crunching his nose.

Lizette rolled beneath the beast, slashing at its belly, then came out on the other side of the creature and swung again, slicing into the bird's other wing.

Alaysia landed another solid blow to the rider's face, pummeling it in its nose and mouth.

Lizette slashed at the creature's leg, cutting deep, slicing through flesh and bone with the fire sword. The acrid smell of burning flesh flared out in a cloud of stench around them.

The Seeker Destroyer staggered, then fell to its side.

"Come on!" Alaysia shouted at Lizette.

Lizette and Alaysia whirled away from the fallen beast and raced for the others. "Go!" Alaysia shouted at Rin and Joktala as they neared them. "Get out!"

Alaysia reached Joktala's side first and pushed him and Rin through the dwindling hole, her momentum propelling her through the hole right behind them. "I said move it!"

T'rok scrambled over the fallen debris in his haste to catch up with the others, the weapons pouch secured over his shoulder. The pouch was heavy for his small size so it was a struggle for him to move quickly with it. He neared the unmoving Seeker Destroyer and started to run past its body, but suddenly the Seeker Destroyer rider reached out and grabbed him! T'rok screamed!

Lizette turned to see—

—T'rok holding his little hands out towards her, his leg caught in the clutches of the Seeker Destroyer rider, his wide eyes filled with fear.

Lizette quickly glanced at the shrinking hole, stared at it for a moment, then turned back to race towards T'rok and the Seeker Destroyer. "Let him go!" Lizette kicked the Seeker Destroyer rider in the face, crunching bone with her boot, and yanked T'rok free of its grip.

She pulled the Gatherer to her chest with her free gloved hand and they raced back to the shrinking hole. T'rok clutched tightly at the weapons pouch with one hand and at Lizette's shirt with the other. As they reached the hole, Lizette pushed T'rok through the dwindling exit, shoving him hard through the fading swirling light.

ASHENWALL - OUTSIDE WORZON HOLE - NIGHT

T'rok tumbled out of the Worzon hole. He saw Joktala and Alaysia hovering over Rin as he lay on the ground near the hole next to her. Alaysia was busy tending to Rin's wounds, still in the shape of a Volgarian.

Around them, the sounds of battle filled the air as the freed Takans battled their Volgarian captors. Several buildings were deeply aflame in the near distance, thick plumes of black smoke swirling up into the sky. Far more Takans were visible than Volgarians at this point, so it was very apparent that the Takans would win this day.

Rin glanced up at T'rok through pain-filled eyes. "Where's Lizette? Did she come through?"

T'rok pointed to the dwindling entrance to the Worzon hole. The rope-like tendrils that were anchoring the hole in place began to shake, working themselves free of the ground.

"No..." His face filling with pure fear, Rin staggered to his feet. He hurled himself at the shrinking hole again and again but was roughly thrown back by the force of the collapsing hole. The dizzying swirl of lights was now only a one-way exit. "I can't get in!"

The Worzon hole opening became smaller and smaller. The anchoring tendrils were now free of the ground; they started to shrivel and dry up, quickly losing any kind of substance.

Suddenly, a round, blood-stained object came

hurtling through the Worzon hole. It hit the ground and rolled right up to them. Rin stared with wide eyes at—

—the severed head of the Seeker Destroyer rider, its neck blackened and charred, its black-and-red streaked eyes staring blankly but still somehow filled with an ominous evil.

"Rin!" It was Lizette's voice, coming from within the collapsing Worzon hole. It was faint, but it was her.

Rin looked towards the Worzon hole, towards the faint voice calling from its darkening depths and saw—

—a slender Human hand clad in a glove emerge from the collapsing Worzon hole.

"Rin!"

"Lizette!" Rin reached out with desperate fingers, making contact with Lizette's gloved hand. They held on for a brief moment, clinging desperately to each other as the Worzon hole opening became smaller and smaller. Then the glove that Rin gripped suddenly flattened as Lizette pulled her arm back away from the small opening. "Rin!" Her voice faded away.

"Lizette!" Rin clutched at the empty air where Lizette's fingers had been, crying out for her again and again, his other hand holding the empty glove.

The Worzon hole opening continued to dwindle, continued to shrink. And now the Worzon hole itself, free of its anchoring, began to rise, began to slowly drift away. Within moments it was dozens of feet in the air, continuing to climb and drift.

Rin could only watch in terror as it moved farther and farther away from him. "Lizette!"

T'rok held up the weapons pouch towards Joktala, but Joktala made no move to take it as he was too preoccupied with watching the terror continue to rise in Rin's face. T'rok slowly lowered the pouch.

EDGE OF BLACK WOODS - DAY

Joktala and Alaysia, now back in Takan form, stood near Rin, watching him study the Black Woods before him. The afternoon air was calm, the two suns casting a warm light over them. "We could use your help," Joktala said. "Ashenwall's gone, but there's already been reports of more than twenty battles against the Volgarians. Some Humans are siding with us, some with the Volgarians. I hope the Scitites just stay out of it, but I doubt they will since some of them had been helping the Volgarians. I'm not sure who the PowderKeepers will side with. Maybe some of us. Maybe all of us. Maybe none of us." Joktala paused. "It's going to stay ugly for a very long time, I think."

Rin was silent, re-adjusting his backpack. He flipped a dagger in his hand and slid it smoothly into its sheath at his waist.

"Are you sure you want to do this?" Joktala asked.

"They said a Worzon hole has been spotted around this area a dozen times in the last three seasons. Maybe it's your friend's hole, maybe it's Hunak's. Maybe he can help me," Rin said.

"What if it's not the same Worzon hole? What if you run into another one of those big fat bastards?" Joktala asked.

"I have to find Lizette. I can still hear her calling out to me." Rin glanced at the glove he had tucked behind his belt. Lizette's glove.

"Maybe you just think you feel her because of what the PowderKeeper did to you," Alaysia said. She hesitated, but then said what was on her mind. "Maybe… she's… gone."

Rin shook his head. "No. I'm going to find her. I have to. She's part of me now." A tear fell down Rin's cheek, the small droplet of sorrow sliding down his face. He quickly wiped at his cheek, not knowing what was trickling down on his face. He looked at the wet smear on his fingers, amazed by the sight. He looked back up at his friends. "She is me. I am her."

Joktala nodded. He held out his arm to Rin and they locked forearms in the Takan greeting of hello. And goodbye. They embraced and Joktala put his mouth to Rin's ear. "She's still alive," he whispered to him. "I've seen her. I don't know where she is, but I have seen her."

Rin nodded and clutched his friend tightly, then pulled back. "Don't kill yourself with all that." Rin pointed to the sack at Joktala's feet, a sack overflowing with sweet leaves.

"I can quit anytime I want," Joktala said.

Rin grinned wryly at his friend.

"Goodbye, Rin," Alaysia said.

Rin turned to Alaysia. They embraced. "I guess you really do need to find yourself," she said softly.

"Yeah, I guess I do. Goodbye, Alaysia." Rin pulled back from the embrace, then turned away from his friends and stepped into the Black Woods, disappearing into the thick shadows.

Joktala and Alaysia stared at the dark woods for a long moment, then turned away.

RIVERBANK NEAR FALLNG STREAM - DAY

Joktala and Alaysia walked along a riverbank on their way back to their village. Joktala suddenly stopped at the river's edge and looked at the closed sack in his hands. He sighed a slow sigh and then hurled the bag into the current, watching it float downstream in the direction they had come from.

Alaysia took his hand in hers and kissed his cheek. "I'm proud of you."

Joktala smiled and squeezed her hand. They continued walking upstream. "Today we rest. We've got a lot of battles in our future, but today we rest."

They continued walking, enjoying the afternoon sun.

"Now about these Human females…" Alaysia said.

Unseen by Alaysia, Joktala glanced over his shoulder and saw T'rok pulling the bag out of the river. The Gatherer glanced up and waved its little furry hand at Joktala before scampering away with the sack.

"...that will stop," Alaysia said, finishing her thought.

Joktala smiled at T'rok, then turned back to Alaysia. His smile grew and he could not help but start to break out into a song. "I'm gonna get some Takan tonight. She'll be—"

Alaysia's hand transformed into stone and began squeezing Joktala's fingers. Hard.

Joktala winced. "Hey! Okay, okay. I'll stop. I'll stop."

The two continued walking. Joktala smiled as a thought struck him. "Now that you can control some of your transformations, maybe you can turn into a sexy Volgarian wench. Maybe—"

Alaysia squeezed even harder.

"Okay, I'll stop! I'll stop!" Joktala wailed.

The two Takans walked on into the distance, Joktala still yelping in pain as they disappeared on the horizon.

Death Gems
Book One
"Soul Stealers"

Soul Stealers choose to use the dark powers of the death gems to steal the souls of innocent victims and use their life-forces to escape death. Junto Kral and his group of Extractors are determined to rid their world of this deadly menace -- but as they learn more about the underbelly of these forces, they realize just how overwhelming their job truly is...

Jack is also the creator and author of the **Land of Fright™** series and the **Spine-Tinglers™** series.

Read on to learn more about these exciting series!

LAND OF FRIGHT

The Land of Fright™ is a place where the dark side of the imagination roams free. It is a mysterious land shrouded in secrecy. It is a massive realm filled with frights from the ancient worlds of yesteryear, a region where modern marvels lurk and run amok, a territory where future fears come into being before their time. It is a world of spine-tingling short stories filled with the strange, the eerie, and the weird. Some of the story realms you visit will intrigue you. Some of them may unsettle you. Some of them may even titillate and amuse you. We hope many of them will give you delicious chills along your journey. The Land of Fright™ encompasses the vast expanse of time and space. You will visit the world of the Past in Ancient Rome, Medieval England, the old West, World War II, and others yet to be explored. You will find many tales that exist right here in the Present, tales filled with modern lives that have taken a turn down a darker path. You will travel into the Future to tour strange new worlds and interact with alien societies, or to just take a peek at what tomorrow may bring.

Illustrated versions of some Land of Fright™ stories, which are called Fright Bites™, are also available.

Land of Fright™ terrorstories contained in Collection I:

#1 - Whirring Blades: A simple late-night trip to the mall for a father and his son turns into a struggle for survival when they are attacked by a deadly swarm of toy helicopters.

#2 - The Big Leagues: A scorned young baseball player shows his teammates he really knows how to play ball with the best of them.

#3 - Snowflakes: In the land of Frawst, special snowflakes are a gift from the gods, capable of transferring the knowledge of the Ancients. A young woman searches the skies with breathless anticipation for her snowflake, but finds something far more dark and dangerous instead.

#4 - End of the Rainbow: In Medieval England, a warrior and his woman find the end of a massive rainbow that has filled the sky and discover the dark secret of its power.

#5 - Trophy Wives: An enigmatic sculptor meets a beautiful woman whom he vows will be his next subject. But things may not turn out the way he plans...

#6 - Die-orama: A petty thief finds out that a WWII model diorama in his local hobby shop holds much more than just plastic vehicles and plastic soldiers.

#7 - Creature in the Creek: A lonely young woman finds her favorite secluded spot inhabited by a monster from her past.

#8 - The Emperor of Fear: In ancient Rome, two coliseum workers encounter a mysterious crate containing an unearthly creature. Just in time for the next gladiator games…

#9 - The Towers That Fell From The Sky: Two analysts race to uncover the secret purpose of the giant alien towers that have thundered down out of the skies.

#10 - God Save The Queen: An exterminator piloting an ant-sized robot faces the queen of a nest he has been assigned to destroy.

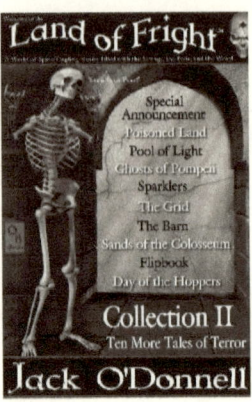

Land of Fright™ terrorstories contained in Collection II:

#11 - Special Announcement: A fraud investigator discovers the disturbing truth behind the messages on a community announcement board.

#12 - Poisoned Land: Savage hunters patrol the Poisoned Lands, demanding appeasement from the three survivors trapped in a surrounded building. How far will each one of them go to survive?

#13 - Pool of Light: A mysterious wave of dark energy from space washes over the Earth, trapping a woman and her friends in pools of light. Beyond the edges of the light, deep pockets of darkness hold much more than just empty blackness.

#14 - Ghosts of Pompeii: A woman on a tour of Italy with her son unwittingly awakens the ghosts of Pompeii.

#15 - Sparklers: A child's sparkler opens a doorway to another dimension and a father must enter it to save his family and his neighborhood from the ominous threat that lays beyond.

#16 - The Grid: An interstellar salvage crew activates a mysterious grid on an abandoned vessel floating in space, unleashing a deadly force.

#17 - The Barn: An empty barn beckons an amateur photographer to step through its dark entrance, whispering promises of a once-in-a-lifetime shoot.

#18 - Sands of the Colosseum: A businessman in Rome gets to experience the dream of a lifetime when he visits the great Colosseum — until he finds himself standing on the arena floor.

#19 - Flipbook: A man sees a dark future of his family in jeopardy when he watches the tiny animations of a flipbook play out in his hand.

#20 - Day of the Hoppers: Two boys flee for their lives when their friendly neighborhood grasshoppers turn into deadly projectiles.

Land of Fright™ terrorstories contained in Collection III:

#21 - The Prospector: In the 1800's, a lonely prospector finds the body parts of a woman as he pans for gold in the wilds of California.

#22 - The Boy In The Yearbook: Two middle-aged women are tormented by a mysterious photograph in their high school yearbook.

#23 - Shot Glass: A man discovers the shot glasses in his great-grandfather's collection can do much more than just hold a mouthful of liquor.

#24 - The Champion: An actor in a medieval renaissance re-enactment show becomes the unbeatable champion he has longed to be.

#25 - Hitler's Graveyard: American soldiers in WWII uncover a nefarious Nazi plan to resurrect their dead heroes so they can rejoin the war.

#26 - Out of Ink: Colonists on a remote planet resort to desperate measures to ward off an attack from wild alien animals.

#27 - Dung Beetles: Mutant dung beetles attack a family on a remote Pennsylvania highway. Yes, it's as disgusting as it sounds.

#28 - The Tinies: A beleaguered office worker encounters a strange alien armada in the sub-basement of his office building.

#29 - Hammer of Charon: In ancient Rome, it is the duty of a special man to make sure gravely wounded gladiators are given a quick death after a gladiator fight. He serves his position quietly with honor. Until they try to take his hammer away from him…

#30 - Pharaoh's Cat: In ancient Egypt, the pharaoh is dying. His trusted advisors want his favorite cat to be buried with him. The cat has other plans…

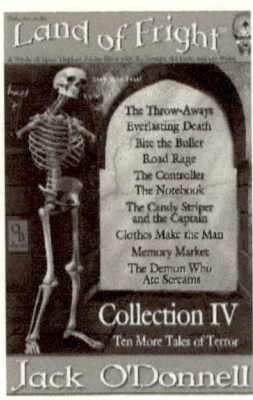

Land of Fright™ terrorstories contained in Collection IV:

#31 - The Throw-Aways: A washed-up writer of action-adventure thrillers is menaced by the ghosts of the characters he has created.

#32 - Everlasting Death: The souls of the newly deceased take on solid form and the Earth fills with immovable statues of death...

#33 - Bite the Bullet: In the Wild West, a desperate outlaw clings to a bullet cursed by a Gypsy... because the bullet has his name on it.

#34 - Road Rage: A senseless accident on a rural highway sets off a frightening chain of events.

#35 - The Controller: A detective investigates a bank robbery that appears to have been carried out by a zombie.

#36 - The Notebook: An enchanted notebook helps a floundering author finish her story. But the unnatural fuel that stokes the power of the mysterious writing journal leads her down a disturbing path...

#37 - The Candy Striper and the Captain: American WWII soldiers in the Philippines scare superstitious enemy soldiers with corpses they dress up to look like vampire victims. The vampire bites might be fake, but what comes out of the jungle is not...

#38 - Clothes Make the Man: A young man steals a magical suit off of a corpse, hoping some of its power will rub off on him.

#39 - Memory Market: The cryptic process of memory storage in the human brain has been decoded and now memories are bought and sold in the memory market. But with every legitimate commercial endeavor there comes a black market, and the memory market is no exception...

#40 - The Demon Who Ate Screams: A young martial artist battles a vicious demon who feeds on the tormented screams and dying whimpers of his victims.

Land of Fright™ terrorstories contained in Collection V:

#41 - The Hatchlings: A peaceful barbecue turns into an afternoon of terror for a suburban man when the charcoal briquets start to hatch!

#42 - Virgin Sacrifice: A professor of archaeology is determined to set the world right again using the ancient power of Aztec sacrifice rituals.

#43 - Smog Monsters: The heavily contaminated air in Beijing turns even deadlier when unearthly creatures form within the dense poison of its thick pollution.

#44 - Benders of Space-Time: A young interstellar traveler discovers the uncomfortable truth about the Benders, the creatures who power starships with their ability to fold space-time.

#45 - The Picture: A young soldier in World War II shows his fellow soldiers a picture of his beautiful fiancé during the lulls in battle. But this seemingly harmless gesture is far from innocent...

#46 - Black Ice: A vicious dragon is offered a great gift — a block of black ice to soothe the fire that burns its throat and roars in its belly. Too bad the dragon has never heard of a Trojan dwarf...

#47 - Artist Alley: At a comic book convention, a seedy comic book publisher sees himself depicted in a disturbing series of artist drawings.

#48 - Dead Zone: A yacht gets caught adrift in the dead zone in the Gulf of Mexico, trapped in an area of the sea that contains no life. What comes aboard the yacht from the depths of this dead zone in search of food cannot really be considered alive...

#49 - Cemetery Dance: A suicidal madman afraid to take his own life attempts to torment a devout Christian man into killing him.

#50 - The King Who Owned the World: A bored barbarian king demands he be brought a new challenger. But who can you find to battle a king who owns the world.

Land of Fright™ terrorstories contained in Collection VI:

#51 - Zombie Carnival: Two couples stumble upon a zombie-themed carnival and decide to join the fun.

#52 - Going Green: Drug runners trying to double cross their boss get a taste of strong voodoo magic.

#53 - Message In A Bottle: A bottle floats onto the beach of a private secluded island with an unnerving message trapped inside.

#54 - The Chase: In 18th century England, a desperate chase is on as a monstrous beast charges after a fleeing wagon, a wagon occupied by too many people...

#55 - Who's Your Daddy?: A lonely schoolteacher is disturbed by how much all of the students in her class look alike. A visit by a mysterious man sheds some light on the curious situation.

#56 - Beheaded: In 14th century England, a daughter vows revenge upon those who beheaded her father. She partners with a lascivious young warlock to restore her family's honor.

#57 - Hold Your Breath: A divorced mother of one confronts the horrible truth behind the myth of holding one's breath when driving past a cemetery.

#58 - Viral: What makes a civilization fall? Volcanoes, earthquakes, or other forces of nature? Barbarous invasions or assaults from hostile forces? Decline from within due to decadence and moral decay? Or could it be something more insidious?

#59 - Top Secret: A special forces agent confronts the villainous characters from his past, but discovers something even more dangerous. Trust.

#60 - Immortals Must Die: There is no more life force left in the universe. The attainment of immortality has depleted the world of available souls. So what do you do if you are desperate to have a child?

The Spine-Tinglers™ series
by Jack O'Donnell

I don't know who I am, or where I came from. All I know is that I can see things and hear things. I have no physical presence, yet I am somehow able to travel through space and time and witness untold events happening all around me. I suppose some of you will label me as a ghost, but that's not truly accurate as I have no recollection of ever being alive, no childhood memories, no remembrances of any traumatic life events that might be keeping me trapped in this world. Nor do I feel as if I am a manifestation of a dead person. I leave no shadowy trace. I am shapeless, formless. Don't get me wrong. Ghosts do exist, as I have seen them. I am just not one of them.

For the most part, all I can do is watch and listen and report back to you what I have seen and heard. I can enter a body and experience feelings and emotions, yet the owner of the body never feels my presence; I don't do this very often, as the feeling is unsettling and mostly unpleasant. Which again is odd in that I have no sense of a body, no sense of a brain, yet somehow I can still feel uncomfortable in certain situations. I do not know where this sense of feeling comes from, yet I can't deny it can affect me. I am as perplexed in trying to explain my current state of what could be called existence as I am sure you are in trying to comprehend it.

I seem to be drawn to those events that have a sinister side to them, a darkness. Perhaps it is my mission to shine some light on that darkness, to reveal the truth that is hidden in those dusky shadows. Perhaps I am here to warn you of what really exists in the world around you, make you a little more aware of the mysteries that often hide shrouded in the bliss of ignorance. I don't really know. All I know is that I am compelled to chronicle what I have observed, what I have heard, what I have felt, and share those experiences with you. Here are the latest stories I felt compelled to chronicle...

The Scarecrow - Spine-Tinglers™ #1

Beware what grows in the corn!

Hideous monsters borne of the blood of the Civil War follow the commands of a demonic scarecrow bent on preserving the sanctity of her crop.

Metamorphosis - Spine-Tinglers™ #2

Beware what lurks in Nektala's Tomb!

Archaeologists unearth the tomb of a mysterious Egyptian ruler and unwittingly discover a secret that threatens to transform all of humanity.

ABOUT JACK O'DONNELL

Jack grew up on Jack Kirby comics, Creature Features, Godzilla movies, Stephen King, Andre Norton, Edgar Rice Burroughs, Don Pendleton, and a smorgasbord of science fiction and fantasy books.

He is the co-producer and co-screenwriter of Stephen King's The Night Flier, based on Stephen King's story.

Visit Jack O'Donnell's author page on Amazon to see his other published works at: **www.amazon.com/Jack-ODonnell/e/B00P43NP00**.

Please also visit the ODONNELL BOOKS bookstore on Amazon to see all of the other books published by ODONNELL BOOKS available at: **www.amazon.com/odonnellbooks**.

If you enjoyed this book, or any of his other works, please take the time to leave a review. Your feedback is greatly appreciated!

Thanks for reading!